Dazzer
Plays On

Steve May

Mammoth

First published in Great Britain in 2000 by Mammoth,
an imprint of Egmont Children's Books Limited
239 Kensington High Street, London W8 6SA

Text copyright © 2000 Steve May
Cover illustrations copyright © 2000 Matt Eastwood

The right of Steve May and Matt Eastwood to be identified as the author
and cover illustrator of this work have been asserted by them in accordance
with the Copyright, Designs and Patents Act 1988

ISBN 0 7497 3431 0

10 9 8 7 6 5 4 3 2 1

A CIP catalogue record for this title is available from the British Library

Typeset by Avon Dataset Ltd, Bidford on Avon, Warwickshire
Printed in Great Britain by Cox & Wyman Ltd, Reading, Berkshire

Special thanks to the strong back four of Jim Lacey, Andy Pinner, Charley Molton and Stuart Bird, without whose contributions Dazzer would not have reached the present pitch.

Contents

1
Danny

One summer, we moved in next door to Danny and his mum.

Danny wasn't called Dazzer then.

My mum said, 'Oh, I was chatting to the woman next door and she's got a boy the same age as you.'

I said, 'I know, he's in my tutor, his name's Danny, he's a nutter.'

'Don't talk like that. I said you'd go round and play with him.'

'Mum, I'm too old to go and play with anyone.'

'Well, go round and say hello.'

So I did.

Their house was clean but it was cluttered with old trash, stuff that looked like it should have been thrown out years ago, and it had this faint musty smell, like mothballs.

'Go straight up,' said Danny's mum. 'He's in his

bedroom playing. He will be pleased to see you.'

I went up the stairs. All the way up the stairs were boxes, cardboard boxes, with cheap ornaments in them and newspaper and a mirror and pictures and stuff like that. Like it was them who just moved in.

I went into Danny's room. He didn't see me at first. He was playing a game. He had this pair of socks rolled up into a ball. He put the sockball down on the floor, carefully. Then he stepped back and hunched himself and growled, then he ran up and kicked the socks as hard as he could, so they bobbled along the floor towards his bed. Then, he jumps over the socks, turns round, picks them up, throws them at himself, and he dives on to the bed and shoves the socks away, like they're a snake and he's Indiana Jones, and he's shouting, 'Save! Save! Save!'

Then he saw me.

His face lit up. He offered the socks to me.

'You want to play, too?'

OK, I did play. It was a stupid game, but it made him happy. He called it sockball. We used to play it a lot that winter, when it was too foul to play outside. I'd lob the socks in the air and he'd throw himself about on the bed, trying to save them. He was such a lump, it sounded like the bed was going to go through the floor. But, his mum didn't seem to mind.

That was sockball.

It still makes my toes curl thinking about it.

Danny-ball we played outside. Round the side of his house there was a sideway with a space for a car but they didn't have a car, and it was covered with corrugated iron, and we played Danny-ball in there.

Danny-ball was a silly game. I'm glad no one saw us. One against one, and we used a plastic ball with holes in it, so it didn't do any damage. Danny liked me to commentate, too. I did it once, and then after that he pestered me to do like a TV commentary: 'Here comes Danny down the left wing, beats one man, crosses to the centre, and Chris heads it in for England.'

I felt stupid doing it but no one could hear. No one was ever going to know.

Danny-ball wasn't proper football, because I played slow-motion. That gave him a chance.

You can play Danny-ball any time of year, even when it's dark, 'cos there's a light bulb outside the kitchen door. Even when it's wet, 'cos you've got the corrugated iron roof.

Danny pestered me to play all the time, but I was busy. I was playing in the school team. I was captain in the second year, and the third year.

Danny. He is mad about football. But, he is seriously rubbish.

When he runs up to a ball, he trots up with little steps, like he's scared it's going to run away from him, and he keeps his feet close together, and he always keeps both feet behind the ball, so when he kicks it's a weedy little dig with his toes, like you see little dogs do on the beach.

He's very slow, and he's clumsy, and when he plays he sort of hunches over, like The Hulk, with his head down and his elbows out like a bear, and he stumbles and he growls. I don't think he knows he's doing it.

That's like his faces.

Danny makes these faces. Not all the time. When he's bored, or tired, or stressed, he sort of stretches his face and wides out his eyes, like a yawn but he's got his mouth shut. Danny's faces get him into trouble sometimes, 'cos the teachers think he's doing it to take the mickey and kids think he's a nutter.

I had my own friends. When they came round to my house, I never mentioned Danny or Danny-ball.

Especially I never mentioned sockball. Like Danny didn't exist next door.

This one time, Mitch and Pete were round and we were in my bedroom playing some board-game. Pete said, 'What's that noise?' He went and looked out the window. Mitch went too, but I stayed where I was 'cos I knew what the noise was. It was a sort of grunting and then *slap-slap*, *slap-slap*.

'Look!' goes Pete, pointing.

Sure enough, down in the sideway next door there's Danny trying to play Danny-ball. On his own. Throwing the ball against the wall, then trying to head it back against the gate (which is the goal).

'What's he doing?' sputters Mitch.

'Oh,' I said, all casual, 'he does it all the time.'

They watched him for a bit, then we played some other board-game or something, then *dri-i-i-i-ing*, the doorbell.

I knew it was Danny 'cos when he rings the doorbell it stays rung. He rings it till the battery runs flat and you can hear the clapper on the bell.

I had to answer it.

Otherwise my mum would go and then she'd ask Danny in and say, why don't you let Danny play too?

Sure enough, it was Danny.

'Hi,' I said.

'Play Danny-ball?' Danny asks.

'No, I can't.'

Danny's looking past me, up the stairs. Mitch and Pete are there, hanging on the banister, craning down.

Danny says, 'Play later on?'

'I'll see.'

I could feel four eyes burning into the back of my head.

Danny turns like a tanker and waddles off. I shut the door.

I'm dragging back up the stairs.

'Danny-ball!' goes Mitch.

'That's what he calls it.'

'You don't play with him, do you?'

I snarled back, 'Course I don't. He's nuts.'

'Danny-ball!' sings Pete.

But, thank goodness, that little story didn't spread back to school. By Monday they'd forgotten it.

Danny.

It's not that he isn't all there – just his world goes at a different speed. His world is simple, clear-cut. He doesn't hide what he feels. If he's sad he scowls, if it's funny he laughs. And one thing about Danny, he laughs more than he scowls, whatever happens. And he never cried. Only once, that I saw.

He always came up smiling, whatever you did to him.

And right and wrong, he knew what was and what wasn't. You couldn't make him do a wrong thing and you couldn't make him tell a lie.

So, he was easy to make a fool of, easy to kid along, easy to take the mickey. Teasing Danny wasn't an all-the-time sort of thing at school. Mostly, people left him alone. But every now and then, when there was nothing else to do, when it was stinking hot and the playground was sticky, or freezing cold so the air hurt your hands, we'd sort of drift into it, baiting him.

I joined in, yeah. I admit it. I never started it, but sometimes I joined in.

There were different games you could play on him. Favourite was rubber nails. You tell Danny Mr Stockwell wants rubber nails from Mr Enyon. So he trots off to Mr Enyon and asks for rubber nails, and then everyone laughs. Including Danny, even though he doesn't know what he's laughing about.

And because Danny laughed it wasn't so cruel, and

7

it wasn't so much fun as if he cried. Because he laughed, even the teachers laughed, except Miss Gilbey, but we'll come to that.

I used to have to walk to school with him. I got extra pocket money for that.

As soon as we got to school, I left him by the wall, and went and played footie.

His mum didn't let Danny play footie in the playground at school.

In case he tore his trousers.

He used to sit on the wall and watch. Glaring out from under his eyebrows. Every kick, he was shifting with his shoulders, flapping with his feet, living the game in his head. And if the ball went under the classroom, he used to crawl under there and get it for us.

Which didn't do his trousers much good.

On games afternoon, he used to sweep the leaves and watch.

I think he was happy like that, not playing proper football. I don't think he missed it, 'cos he was so bad, and if he played, everyone picked on him. On Thursday afternoon, when we were playing soccer on the field, you'd see Danny with his black rubbish sack, scuffing along the paths, scraping up litter and growling to himself. Every now and then he'd put his head down and chase a paper bag or a leaf, and scuff a kick at it, and he'd shout, 'Goal!'

The only football Danny played at school was flick football on his desk. He'd roll up a bit of paper and suck it in his mouth and leave it to go hard, and he'd make a goal by opening out his wooden pencil-case, and then his hands take it in turns to flick the ball towards the goal. He concentrates really hard. It's only a small opening in the pencil-case, so he doesn't often score.

If he does score, he shouts out, 'Goal!'

But the teachers don't say anything – Danny's Danny.

Except Miss Gilbey.

2
If you want, you can do

Miss Gilbey was new, and she was our tutor, so she took register and tutor period every Monday morning first thing. She wasn't pretty, she was young and small and neat, and she was so sensible it was scary. We didn't mess with her. Whatever she said, we went along with it – even if we thought it was stupid.

She was the kind of teacher who makes you want to do good things. Makes you want to impress her. But nothing seems to.

Every Monday morning, she set us a topic to write about. Like you do at junior school. It's not like real work, writing. But it's easy, better than trying to write essays about old books, or maths. So we went along with it.

And, because it's not a real lesson, it's only tutor

group, you can have a bit of a laugh, chat a bit, so long as you don't go mad.

This one time, she told us to write about, What I Really Want. She told us, her motto was:

If you want, you can do.

She says it all the time, and the way she says it, it sounds true. She told us all these stories about people who'd really wanted difficult things, like climbing mountains or rescuing shipwrecks, and done it.

Well, we were all writing away, except Danny. He was playing flickball, and all of a sudden his left hand scored and he shouts out, 'Goal!'

Everyone looked and cheered. That's what we do.

Danny sank his head down near his arms, 'cos he's embarrassed. Because, he doesn't shout out on purpose. It just pops out.

Miss Gilbey jumped up from her desk where she'd been sitting and crossed over to Danny.

We all go quiet.

She stands right in front of his desk.

Danny's head sinks lower. With his hands he's trying to close up the pencil-case.

Miss Gilbey asks, 'Why haven't you written anything?'

His head shakes a bit but he doesn't look up.

Miss Gilbey goes stern. 'Why did you shout out?'

Danny looks up. His face goes stretchy. He wides out his eyes like a yawn but he's got his mouth shut.

'Don't make faces at me!' she snaps.

Heather calls out, 'He can't help it, he's not all there.'

Miss Gilbey goes very red round the neck. She swallows hard. She checks the register she's carrying.

'It's Danny, is it?'

He nods, once.

She leans closer.

Now her voice is gentle, soft.

'And why did you shout out?'

'I scored.'

It comes out like a growl. He holds up his finger to show her.

She moves a little further away from him. Asks, 'What did you score?'

'A goal.'

And he holds up the little bit of chewed up paper.

She asks him, 'Do you like football?'

Danny nods.

'Well, then, that's what you can write about, isn't it?'

Danny set to work. He's a slow writer and he presses very hard with his pen. Miss Gilbey came to see how he was getting on. She read it to herself, then she read it out loud to all of us. This is what he'd written:

> *What I want is to score a goal because I never scored a real goal with posts and a net and wear a proper shirt with colours the ball flies past the goalie's diving and it bulges out the net like a fish in a net and I'm going to stand there and the ball's lying there in the goal and I scored. I want to score a real goal like Chris he's captain he plays with me sometimes.*

By the end of it, Danny's got his arms crossed and he's trying to bury his head into his arms, like a big fat ostrich.

I'm thinking, at least he didn't mention sockball.

Miss Gilbey looks round us.

'Now isn't that wonderful?'

We all know we've got to think it's wonderful even

if it isn't, because she says so. Heather Field says, 'It really captures the excitement of the game, doesn't it?'

The rest of us nod.

Miss Gilbey says, 'Of course, it needs some tidying to be made into good sentences, but –'

Miss Gilbey pauses. She turns back to Danny.

'So, haven't you ever scored a goal?'

'Only a sock goal.'

'What's a sock goal?'

'You kick a sock goal so it goes under the bed.'

Everyone sniggers.

Except me. This is getting a bit close to home.

Miss Gilbey glances round the room.

The sniggers die.

'If you want, you can do,' Miss Gilbey says. 'I bet if you try hard enough, you'll score your goal.'

Bobby pipes up from the back, 'I don't think so, Miss.'

Miss Gilbey turns on him, ice cold, enough to freeze a two-bar fire.

'What do you mean, Bobby?'

'Danny doesn't play any football.'

'Only sockball!' Kenny shouts.

Miss Gilbey ignores Kenny. She's talking to Danny, soft and gentle.

'Why don't you play football?'

Danny says, 'I can't play at school in case it hurts my trousers.'

We all laugh.

Miss Gilbey glares. The laughter stops.

'Who decided that?'

'Mr Stockwell said so.'

'Well,' she says, 'we'll have to see about that.'

3
Mr Stockwell

Mr Stockwell was geography, but he thought he knew all about football. He picked the teams. There was this one kid from our school called Alan Pearce about a million years ago who played for England schoolboys. Once. And that qualified Mr Stockwell as Manager of the Century.

He kept saying things like:

'When Alan Pearce was skipper, Kingsley was a proper team.'

Or:

'When Alan Pearce was skipper, Kingsley wouldn't have given away that goal.'

He used to referee the games in these old-fashioned galoshes and a long mac. The galoshes were so he didn't have to take his shiny shoes off and so he didn't get muddy. But on match days, he wore a proper smart track suit.

Games was Thursday afternoon, and school matches were Saturdays. We wear school kit for Saturdays – Stockwell keeps that, in a big bag – but on Thursdays you wear your own. The first team wear these red tie-on bibs. They're cheap and a bit tacky but there's still something special about it, tying your bib on. 'Cos there's only ten bibs and if you get given one it means you're in the team.

The reserves try hard but they're not very good. And even if you are any good, it's tough to break into the team.

Stockwell picked the team at the beginning of the year and it hasn't changed much since. It hasn't changed that much since the first year, the first year we were at the school.

Everyone knows who's the best player and the next best, and so on.

I'm the captain and then Bobby's the next best player after me. He was captain in the first year and he hates me.

We've had a dreadful season, so far, in the league. Played 10, drawn 3, lost 7. We've lost the last 6 in a row.

So, this Thursday afternoon we got changed for

football, as usual. All except Danny. As usual. He was out with his broom, doing the leaves.

Bobby shouts out, 'Here, look who's coming.'

We crowded up to the window.

Picking her way along the muddy path is Miss Gilbey. Walking along beside her, is Danny. Head down, broom in both hands. She's got her hand on Danny's shoulder, steering him along.

'Looks like he's under arrest,' said Kenny.

Stockwell saw them coming.

Drew himself erect.

Moustache bristling, eyes bright and small in his head.

I pulled my socks on any old how and my boots, so I could get outside quick.

'But why?' Miss Gilbey is using her freezer voice. 'The boy obviously loves the game, why won't you let him play?'

'He's happy as he is. No one bothers him. He lives in his own world.'

Danny glances out from under his eyebrows. Miss Gilbey doesn't take any notice of him.

'He should be allowed to live in the same world as everyone else.'

'It'll only cause trouble. He'll get picked on.'

'That's your job to prevent.'

'His mother doesn't like him playing.'

'There's lots of things mothers don't like. If we paid attention to all of them there wouldn't be any lessons at all.'

Stockwell nods his head. He's smiling. A superior, I-know-best smile.

'Look, he can play any time he likes, so far as I'm concerned.'

'Let him play today then.'

'OK, but I guarantee you it'll end in tears.'

Miss Gilbey's eyes are blazing. 'It had better not,' she says. Then she bends over to Danny and says, 'Have a lovely game. Score that goal!'

And off she goes.

Stockwell is shaking his head.

I'm thinking, there's only one football here, and it's Danny. Who is standing there still as a statue, with his shoulders hunched, glaring out from under his eyebrows. The broom's tight in his hands.

Stockwell reaches out, grabs the broom, tugs it. Danny hangs on, won't let go.

Stockwell hunches down so he's looking Danny in

the eye as far as possible. He talks loud and slow.

'You're going to play football, aren't you? You don't need a broom to play football. Unless you're going to be sweeper.'

Everyone giggles.

Danny lets go of the broom.

Stockwell takes it, slings it off towards the tool hut. It clatters against the wooden wall.

'Now,' he says. 'We'd better get you kitted out.'

4
The C game

Stockwell sent Moxy down with Danny to the lost property cupboard. Danny came back wearing: a white shirt gone pink in the wash, so tight all his folds of fat stood out in rolls; tiny, skimpy black shorts, extra tight round the tops of his legs; one green sock, one red sock; and old trainers. The left one had a gap at the toe.

'OK,' said Stockwell, 'looks like you're ready for action. I know you'll soon be playing centre forward for England, but we'll start you off in the C game.'

There's four groups on a Thursday: A, B, C and D. A is the school team, B is the reserves, C and D is the rest. The team and the reserves do some training and then we have a practice match. C and D don't do any training. They just have a kickabout on a small makeshift pitch behind one of our goals.

They don't have proper goals, they have these wooden skittle sort of blocks for posts, and they don't have a proper ball, they have a really light plastic thing.

The C versus D games are a complete shambles.

It's all the roughs, and the no-hopers, plus the non-triers, plus the weeds and the lazy kids. There's a few keeners, but they are seriously rubbish.

If you're any good, it's like a death sentence getting sent to the C game. You get dragged down to their level. The keeners rush about like headless chickens, and the rest jog about, just enough to keep warm. Not even that. Some of them stand about with their hands in their pockets. Waiting for it to be over.

Stockwell got them kicked off.

We were doing dribbling round beanbags.

I couldn't help watching to see how Danny got on.

Not too bad. To start with. Course, he wasn't getting anywhere near the ball, but he was lumbering round, trying his hardest, growling and stumbling. He got muddy where he fell down. But he was smiling and frowning and grunting and doing stretchy face.

It was OK.

We started doing give-and-go in groups of four.

There's a burst of laughter from the C game.

Howling laughter, like you do when it's not funny.

Danny's standing in the middle of the pitch with the ball at his feet. Standing like he's lost, looking round.

Stockwell bawls over, 'Danny, play on, get on with the game!'

Stockwell hates the C game.

Danny scuffed at the ball, it rolled away, and the C game got going again.

I asked Pete, 'What happened there?'

'Just watch.'

I did.

Then it happened again.

Alex Fraser started it.

He waited till Stockwell was way down the other end of our pitch, then he pushed Stanley Farnsworth off the ball, picked it up, and ran over to Danny.

He put the ball down in front of Danny.

Then Alex stretched his face, and wided his eyes, but kept his mouth shut. And, at the same time, he did stupid weedy kicks with his feet and waved his arms above his head with the wrists limp.

As soon as he did it, all the others joined in.

Danny's standing there like a lemon.

BJ's right behind him, prodding him and then dancing away, so Danny can't see who's doing it. All these no-hope kids are bursting with laughter but holding it in. It really bugged me, 'cos they're no better than Danny. At least Danny's trying.

Stockwell turns round, and they all stop dancing about and start playing again.

After that, I watched them like a hawk. Because, the next time they did it, I was going to go over and tell Alex Fraser what he can do with his stupid jokes.

I was pretty wound up, I can tell you.

Alex and BJ and Andy Stewart, they're the hard cases in our school. I steer clear of them. They're not in our tutor. They're always bunking off and smoking, and they think it's cool to hang about and they think playing footie's stupid and a waste of time.

But, they leave me alone. Which is one good thing about being school captain. It gives you some cred.

Stockwell is yelling at me.

'Chris, what are you staring at? You're supposed to be training. Just because you're captain, it doesn't mean you're excused. We haven't exactly been doing very well.'

I said to him, 'I think they're picking on Danny.'

'Mind your own business.'

'What if he gets hurt?'

Stockwell's eyes are blazing.

'That's his fault for wanting to play.'

'Is that a crime, sir?'

'You think you're so good, don't you, Chris? Well I'm telling you you're not. You're a very ordinary player. When Alan Pearce was skipper, we wouldn't have lost six games in a row –'

Then this shout went up.

5
Blowsir!

I spun round, thought it was Alex Fraser again, but no.

There, picking her way in her neat little shoes through the mud, out to the pitch, is Miss Gilbey. Looking around like she's just landed on a foreign planet.

Stockwell was over to the touchline like a flash, and stood with her. He pointed this way and that like an army sergeant. He puffed his chest out.

The C game, you never saw such a change. It was like ballroom dancing with her there watching. All polite and interested.

She was pretty chatty with Stockwell. I don't know what she was saying, but she was saying it for ages. Her mouth was going like a rabbit.

Stockwell blew his whistle. Waved his arms. Ran on to the C game pitch.

The no-hopers are trooping off, moving quicker than they've done all afternoon.

Danny trots along with the rest of them, a big smile on his face.

'Hold on,' shouts Stockwell, 'I didn't say go, did I?'

They stop, start moaning.

'Come on,' goes Stockwell, catching the ball and trotting towards one of the goals. 'It's a penalty.'

'Why?' BJ snarls.

'Because I said so,' says Stockwell.

'It's time to go home,' goes Andy Stewart.

Stockwell ignores him.

He puts the ball about five metres from the blue skittle goal. He looks round, calls out, 'Come on, Danny, you take the kick.'

Danny's standing there, not moving. Like he's paralysed.

'Come on, Danny,' goes Stockwell, briskly briskly.

'Come on, Danny,' goes Alex Fraser, in a silly voice.

Giggles.

In goal, is Pudge Morgan. Stockwell makes him play in goal because he's too fat to run much. Pudge is pawing the goal line with his feet, crouching, leaning forward.

Danny v Pudge. What a contest.

Danny walks back about 100 metres, and he looks very determined. His eyes are almost shut, he's concentrating so hard. Now it all goes quiet. Miss Gilbey shouts out, 'Come on, Danny!' She's frozen there with her hands clasped on her chest, and a puzzled look on her face.

There's a funny feeling in the air.

We all know what Miss Gilbey wants, and most of us, we want what she wants, 'cos we want the world to be like she says it is. But, somehow, we know something's going to go wrong.

Danny comes lumbering in, hopping and stepping to keep his stride right.

When he gets to the ball, instead of kicking it, he hops right over it.

Pudge is totally fooled. He dives splat in the mud. Stockwell shouts, 'What on earth are you playing at now, Danny?'

Danny turns round and says, 'Did you blow, sir?'

All hell broke loose. Howling and pointing and laughing.

Miss Gilbey was smiling too.

She didn't understand.

Stockwell said, 'Yes I did blow, now please take the penalty in your own time.'

Danny went back a few steps, tippy-toed up to the ball and toe-poked it.

Pudge did a totally unnecessary dive and stopped it.

Stockwell turned to Miss Gilbey.

'See what I mean? He couldn't score a goal if it was ten miles wide and no goalkeeper.'

There was a smile on Stockwell's face as he ran off. A nasty smile.

I walked off. Danny walked just behind me. Miss Gilbey came up to us.

'Well,' she goes, 'did Danny score or not?'

'Not yet,' I said.

'Never mind,' she said, 'I'm sure he will soon.'

And off she trips after Stockwell.

It was wild in the changing hut.

'Blowsir!' calls Bobby.

'Blowsir!' goes someone else.

Then everyone joined in.

They laughed at Danny's shirt, his shorts, his socks,

his daps, his underpants. You name it. And they had plenty of time. Because Danny is a slow and careful dresser.

Danny didn't get upset. He looked more puzzled than anything. Cross between a frown and a grin. Just like he looked when Alex and BJ were teasing him out on the pitch.

I went outside to wait for him.

Heather and some of the girls came out of the girls' hut. They were chatting about Danny and football.

'It's stupid,' Julie Devonshire said, 'stupid letting him play.'

'It's that Miss Gilbey's fault.'

'Yeah, that's right.'

'Interfering.'

Funny how the girls didn't rate Miss Gilbey as much as the boys did.

I said, 'It's Alex and them lot who picked on him.'

Heather did her haughty face. 'Miss Gilbey should have known what was going to happen. She is a teacher. That's what she's paid for.'

And they sauntered off.

I waited for Danny.

Danny didn't talk at all on the way home. He didn't

run or growl or scuff at stones. I didn't know what to say. It was all running through my head. I was angry and irritable, and mad at Miss Gilbey and Stockwell and everyone. I don't know why, but it felt like it was my fault. Danny was bugging me too, with his face like fourpence.

I asked, 'What's up, Danny?'

Danny stopped walking, and I had to stop too. I felt uncomfortable, in case people were looking. He had a big sprawl of mud across his nose and on to his cheek. He said, 'Am I going to score a goal?'

I said, 'You score lots of goals, in Danny-ball and sockball.'

'A proper goal.'

'You might.'

'Miss Gilbey said.'

'Miss Gilbey's very nice but she doesn't know a thing about football.'

I got a tissue out and tried to wipe some of the mud off his face. He stood there, patient like a cow in a field.

Some girls from St Hugh's came up from the other way, so I quickly put the tissue away.

6
Hall ball

Next morning, Miss Gilbey came in very pleased with herself. She asks Danny, 'Have you scored your goal yet?'

He shook his head.

'Never mind,' she says, 'and in fact in some ways that's good, because –'

And she pulls this book out of her bag. It's a proper notebook with hard black covers and a red spine.

'This is going to be your football diary,' she says. She hands him the book. Everyone's craning to see. It's a really smart book.

Danny holds it like This Is Your Life.

'And I'm sure,' she says, 'it'll be a very exciting diary, and very soon you'll have your goal to put in it.'

And she doesn't leave it there.

'Right,' she says, 'I've got a bit of surprise laid on.'

And she made us put our books away and we trooped down to the small hall. Everyone's whispering, wondering what's coming off. The hall's cold. It smells of dinners.

'OK,' says Miss Gilbey. 'We're going to have a game. Danny, you're one captain, Heather, you're the other.'

I gulped.

We all gulped.

Bobby calls out, 'What kind of game is it, Miss?'

'Football, of course.'

Miss Gilbey shows us this ball about the size of a grapefruit. It's not a football. It's got chunky tread on it, and if you squash it it squeaks.

People start muttering.

'That's a baby ball.'

'Heather can't be captain, she's a girl.'

'Chris, he's the captain.'

'Danny's no good.'

Miss Gilbey shushes us with a big blast on her whistle. A yellow whistle on red string.

'I'm in charge, and you'll do what I say.'

Danny picked me, first pick.

I told him to pick Mitch next, but Miss Gilbey interrupted.

'You don't want all boys, do you, Danny? Pick some girls as well.'

It ended up, I don't know, six or seven a side. The rest had to sit on benches and watch.

It was crazy.

I was telling everyone where to go, what position to play, when Miss Gilbey came over.

'Chris, go in goal, please.'

'But I'm not a keeper, I'm midfield.'

'Well, today, you're the goalie. Danny, you be forward.'

And so on. She told everyone where to go.

Then we kicked off.

It was a funny game with the little ball on the hard parquet floor, with tables on their sides for goals, and mixed teams, playing in our socks, in our normal clothes, in the small hall, which is only used for assemblies and dinners.

It wasn't a proper game.

Every time you kicked the ball, it squeaked.

It was obvious what Miss Gilbey wanted. She wanted Danny to score, and that's all she wanted

34

and that's why she was doing it.

He did the best he could, lumbering about, trying to get somewhere near the ball. Not getting near the ball very often. When he did get near it, scuffing at it so it dribbled away sideways.

Miss Gilbey looked puzzled. She kept blowing her whistle and giving free kicks to Danny.

Still he didn't score.

'Right,' she goes. 'Now it's penalties.'

Danny took five penalties, with Heather in goal. Three times he missed the goal completely. The other two she saved. Which wasn't difficult – they were dribbly scuffers.

Danny was starting to go curled up. That's what happens when he knows everyone's looking at him, and he's embarrassed. Hot red face. Like he's curling up so no one can see him.

Miss Gilbey told Heather to stand to one side.

'There you are,' Miss Gilbey says to Danny. 'An open goal.'

Danny missed with his first but then connected with the second. He hit it with his toe, straight along the floor, slap against the table.

The table toppled over, smash down on the floor.

Could have hurt someone.

Everyone cheered, laughing.

'At last,' Heather goes.

Miss Gilbey caught the ball. 'Thank goodness for that,' she said. 'Now, everyone, put your shoes on.'

We trooped back to the classroom.

Miss Gilbey was happy as Larry.

'Right,' she says. 'Danny, it's about time you wrote your football diary.'

He wrote:

> *The ball squeaked, the table fell over, everyone laughed.*

Everyone laughed again when they heard that.

Except Miss Gilbey. She couldn't see what the joke was about.

7
A beautiful idea

On the way home that night, I said to Danny, 'At least you scored.'

He looked at me. 'Not a proper a goal.'

'Do you still want to score a proper goal?'

He nodded, and turned and walked on, his shoulders slumped, his head down. I could tell from his facials, he was thinking very hard.

I was thinking too.

I had this feeling welling up inside me, this idea, this beautiful idea, so I not only get into Miss Gilbey's good books and become a hero, but also save her from being made to look stupid.

It was such a wonderful idea, it bubbled up inside me. I heard Miss Gilbey's voice, '*If you want, you can do,*' and this warm glow started in my stomach and spread its way up through my chest because I could see it suddenly all so clearly.

Danny, trained by me, becomes a good player and scores his goal, and Miss Gilbey is watching, and she comes over to me and says, Chrissy, that's brilliant, I can't thank you enough.

But when I turned and looked at Danny, I couldn't bring myself to put it into words.

He said, 'I'm no good at footie, am I?'

'No, you're garbage.'

'Can I get better at football?'

That was just what I wanted to hear. I said, 'Yes, I think you can get better. If you're prepared to work very hard and do training.'

'And you help me?'

'Of course I help you.'

'And then I score a goal?'

'I don't see why not.'

And, at that moment, I believed it.

I started jogging, jumping.

Danny jogged along behind me, grinning all over his face. Doing little jumps so he hardly left the ground.

Why not?

Why shouldn't it happen?

It caught me like an illness, the enthusiasm. Miss Gilbey's enthusiasm. I was the star player in the school team, I knew all about football, why shouldn't I be able to train Danny up so he could play proper football? OK, maybe he'd never be the greatest player in the world, but I could teach him so he could play on Thursdays and not get laughed at. I'd show BJ and Alex Fraser and those clowns, and I'd show Miss Gilbey, and I'd save her, and I'd show Stockwell! Everyone would like me and think I was cool and we'd win the league too!

8
Kitting out

When we got home I went in and saw Danny's mum.

'Have they been picking on him again?'

'No,' I said, 'Mr Stockwell said he didn't have to play!'

'Danny wants to play football, and Mr Stockwell says I've got to help him.'

Mrs Barker looked doubtful. She didn't ask Danny what he thought. He was sat with his chin crouched over the back of a chair, not looking at us. He was growling, in his throat. I think it was a song.

His mum said, 'I'm not sure that's such a good idea. He's happy as he is. He plays all these games in his head and no one picks on him.'

I said, 'I'm going to train him up so he can play just as good as anyone else.'

She smiles. 'That's very kind of you, but even if it was possible that wouldn't stop people picking on him.

They don't pick on him just because he can't play football.'

I felt like saying, I know that, 'cos I've picked on him myself. But I said, 'I'll stop them picking on him!'

'He has to stand up for himself.'

But the more she said no, the more urgent I got to get the chance. And the longer the argument went on, the surer I was I could do it. I could train him up and I could protect him. I had these pictures in my mind of BJ and Alex Fraser and Andy Stewart trying to make fun of Danny, and me stepping in and saying, you leave him alone. Mess with him, and you mess with me too. I was carried away, I tell you. I was hot with the idea.

I said to Mrs Barker, 'Look, at least let's kit him out in some proper kit and do some training. If it doesn't work, we'll forget all about it.'

'But I can't afford proper kit.'

'Let me worry about that. Surely he deserves a chance?'

For the first time since I got in there, Mrs Barker looks across to Danny. He's staring into space, with his eyes squeezed up.

'OK,' she says, 'but I don't want him getting hurt.'

We didn't tell anyone else about the training.

'Best keep it a secret,' I told Danny. 'Then we'll surprise them!'

Next day, after school, we went into town. We went into the Oxfam shop, the Imperial Cancer shop, and the Cat Protection League shop. They smell funny, those shops, like someone died and the bodies are still out the back.

Danny liked this red Swindon Town shirt, but I told him, that's too sad. We settled on a black and white striped shirt. It said 'Inter Milan' on it. I don't think it was a real Inter Milan shirt but it was OK from a distance. The shorts were black – I don't know what team. They had bits of red on them. But, they were plenty big enough.

The socks were blue but I told him they looked black from a distance.

The boots were tougher. Danny's got big feet – size nine.

Most of the boots in the shops were too small. Danny wanted to buy the first pair he could get his feet into – size eleven, made in about 1959, with huge steel toecaps.

'No, Danny, we've got to find the right size.'

And we did.

In the Cat Protection League. A pair of black Pumas with moulded-on studs, fifty pence including laces and some old stuck-on mud. Danny tried them on and waddled around the shop.

'How do they feel?'

'Great.'

I got down on the floor and felt for his toe, and it seemed about right. And I looked up, and he was standing stock-still, staring off into the distance, with a sort of proud mask of a face, like he was posing for a photo before the cup final.

'Are they a bit on the small side?' the old dear asks who serves in the shop.

'No,' I said, 'they're perfect.'

That night, instead of playing Danny-ball in the sideway, we played passes. We still used the plastic ball with holes, but Danny insisted on wearing full kit, including boots, so he clattered like a horse on the concrete.

I told him, 'We're not playing Danny-ball now. We're not pretending. We're doing things properly.'

We passed that ball backwards and forwards.

'See how many times we can do it.'

I had to be quick. When Danny kicked the ball, it

could go anywhere. By nine o'clock our record was fifteen. I thought that was pretty good.

Next morning was Saturday. It was winter, cold, and the doorbell went about eight am. *Dri-i-i-i-ng.* Danny. On the doorstep. In his new shorts, a woollen jumper hanging out, and old shoes. He had this old football, with no air in it, under his arm and his new boots in a bag over his shoulder. When he got the boots out of the bag, I didn't recognise them. He must have spent all night cleaning and polishing.

He sat in the kitchen while I got dressed. He sat there at the table making faces and growling. It was the first time he'd really been in our house, to sit down. My mum, she was in the kitchen with him. She came up to me and whispered, 'Is he all right?'

I said, 'Sure, he's as normal as you or me. Except when he plays football.'

Danny was keen to get off down the park right away, but I said no.

'We've got to start right at the beginning,' I told him.

He nodded, his face screwed up with concentration.

'We start with knowledge of the game, because there's no point being superfit and having amazing ball skills if you don't know how to use them in an actual match.'

'OK.' He looks serious.

'Question one: what's a goal?'

'A goal's a goal when the ball goes in the goal.'

'Good. Can you punch it in?'

'No. You kick it, or head it.' He kicked and headed at thin air to show me what he meant.

'Which goal do you have to score in?'

Danny thinks for a moment. 'Their goal.'

'Good. And what's offside?'

'Offside's if the ball goes over the line for a throw.'

'No, that's not right.'

Danny looks even more serious.

'Tell me then.'

I took a deep breath. 'Never mind. We'll do that in lesson two.'

9
Serious training

We ran to the park.

I thought, it's OK, it's so early, there won't be anyone there.

Danny was keen but very unfit. I ran along sideways beside him, urging him on.

Danny's got the strangest legs. They're big and they've got no shape. They don't go in and come out at the knee. They go straight up and down and they're solid fat, like lard. They don't ripple. And they're palest white and they go blotchy in the cold, and I expect they rub and go sore.

Sausage legs.

We got started.

Danny wanted to use his ball but it was old and flat and heavy leather. It had green mould on it. You couldn't blow it up. So, we used mine. Not a proper match ball, but it's full size and quite heavy.

We tried passing. It's harder in the park than in the sideway. The park hasn't got any walls. You have to keep running to fetch.

I rolled the ball towards him.

'Now you kick it back to me.'

He tippy-toed a couple of steps towards the ball. Hands perched up on his chest like a hamster. Takes a swing. Scuffs it off the outside of his new boot.

I did it again. He waits, his face bursting with concentration, and then at the last minute he takes a scuff at the ball. Misses it completely.

'OK,' I said, 'let's get back to basics.'

I showed him how to kick a ball.

'You've got to put your left foot beside it and then swing the right foot through so your whole body weight swings through the ball.'

He couldn't grasp that. Or if he did in his head, he couldn't get it from his head down to his legs.

He was all over the place.

So, I set the ball down, and knelt down, and I put his left foot beside it, and held it there, and I said, 'Now kick.'

He kicked.

Gradually he got the hang of it.

47

I made him stand by a jumper. I passed to him, 'You pass back to me.'

He kicked. The ball flew past me.

'Goal!' he shouts.

'That wasn't a goal,' I said, 'that was a bad pass. Now go and get it.'

I showed him how to use the inside of his foot to stroke the ball. He turned his whole leg nearly inside out and leaned back and pushed at the ball like he was doing some old cokey dance. But it worked, sometimes.

'Score a goal now?'

'OK,' I said, 'let's give it a try.'

I put our jumpers down as goalposts, then I got him to stand about a metre from the goal line and I rolled the ball across and he tried to kick it in.

The fourth time, he connected and in it went.

'Yes!' I shouted.

He turned and looked at me, his face twisted up.

'That's not a real goal,' he said.

That bugged me. I said, 'I know it's not a real goal but this is training and it's a start.'

When he'd done that a few times, I made it harder: I went further away, and I got him to start from further

48

away and try and run in. That took him much longer to get the hang of.

'It's all timing,' I told him.

Danny's timing was bad. He never got to the ball at the right moment.

'OK,' I said, 'we'll do some more work on that later. Now let's do some tackling. I've got the ball, I run towards you, you try and get the ball off me.'

He crouches and growls, with his shoulder towards me. I trot towards him, toeing the ball. I'm waiting for him to make a move. He doesn't. I take the ball round him. He's still crouched there.

I stop.

'The idea is, you choose the right moment as I go past, and you stick your foot out and try and kick the ball away from me.'

We tried it again.

I ran straight at him and, at the last moment, tipped the ball to the left and round him. As I went round him, I ran into this huge, hard jelly thing. He'd pushed out with his knee so all his jelly thigh was in my way. It was like running into a padded road block. Down I went.

'Sorry,' he said.

'Don't be sorry,' I said, getting up. 'That was much better.'

'It was a foul,' he goes.

I ignored that. I said, 'Now it's headers.'

He nods, like he's heading an imaginary ball.

'OK,' I said. 'The thing is to get it smack in the middle of your forehead. OK. Let's try.'

I lobbed the ball gently up. Danny did a little one legged jump with his shoulders hunched and his paws up like a hamster, and the ball bounced right off the very topmost top part of his head.

'Forehead, think forehead!'

He tried it again, and again, and again.

No luck.

Off his ear, his chin, his shoulder.

I thought, maybe I'm lobbing the ball too slow.

So, the next one I threw a bit lower. OK, yes, I threw it a bit harder too. I threw it a bit harder, and it went smack right into his face, right on his nose, I suppose.

He crouched down, I ran up to him.

'Are you OK?'

He looks up, nodding, smiling. There's a big blob of mud on his cheek. He says, 'That was better wasn't it?'

I slapped him on the shoulder. 'Much better.'

Danny got up, still holding his face.

Then this voice piped up from behind me, 'Do you fancy a game?'

10
Littlies

There were half a dozen little kiddies, aged about ten or eleven. At the front, with an orange ball under his arm, was the littlest of the littlies. He said, 'We'll play us against you.'

I looked at Danny.

'OK,' I said.

'Great!' buzzed the littlies.

'You can have rush goalies,' the littlest one said.

'Right,' I said to Danny, 'I'll be rush goalie, you be midfield and striker. Just remember what we've been doing.'

He nods.

We start playing.

The little kids are dead keen but they're also overawed, to start with. You only have to run at them and they get out the way, leave you the ball.

I passed to Danny. It hit his legs, ran on, he turned

and chased after it. The kiddies are swarming round him, chasing and trying to get a kick at the ball. Danny runs through them like a bull through a cloud of flies.

'Go on!' I'm shouting.

He's hacking and scuffing and grunting. Two of the kiddies bounce off him. The ball breaks clear, Danny's after it.

'Have a pop!' I shout. Danny takes a big hoof, and the ball slices up in the air, over the goalie, way over the goal, and bounces off towards the trees.

Danny stands there, puzzled.

He doesn't know if it's a goal or not.

'Bad luck,' I shout. 'Over the bar.'

Danny nods, trots off to fetch the ball.

Their skipper, the littlest of these littlies, turns to me with a twisted face and says, 'Is he real?'

'Just you wait,' I said.

Danny brings the ball back, gives it to their keeper.

They come swarming down the pitch.

Danny comes puffing back after them.

The little skipper kid gets the ball and tries to run it in and round me, but I dive down and get the ball and knock him over just to show him it's a real game.

I roll the ball out, set off down the pitch. Danny's

behind me, struggling to keep up. I pass the ball to him, he takes a hack, misses. One of the kiddies darts in, gets the ball, and they swarm back and score, 'cos it's an empty goal.

'Goal!'

'1–0.'

'We are the champions.'

And that was it. Up till then, they thought we were good, they treated us with respect. As soon as they scored, they were all over us.

Danny couldn't tackle.

He couldn't mark.

He was slow getting to the ball.

He couldn't read the game, where the ball was going to go.

He was puffing and panting.

But, he kept trying.

His kicking was a bit better.

The littlies were 5–1 up.

'Thanks for the game,' I said. 'We've got to go.'

'You're not singing any more,' chants one of the littlies.

'So?' I said. 'We were never singing in the first place.'

Walking home, Danny was scuffing at stuff on the pavement.

'We lost, didn't we?' he said.

'You win some you lose some.'

'Was it my fault?'

'No, Danny, it's a team game.'

Pause.

Then he glares at me from under his eyebrows.

'Am I getting any better?'

'Yeah, sure, course you are. But, it's early days.'

I tried to think of something else to say. I said, 'We've got a really tough match this afternoon. Against Northolt. It's the second round of the cup.'

Danny's eyes went wide. 'Am I playing?'

'No, not yet.'

'Oh,' said Danny, 'I thought you wanted me to play.'

'I'd love for you to play, but it's Stockwell who picks the team. He puts the team names up on a sheet in the gym corridor on Friday morning.'

'Oh,' said Danny, 'I didn't look at that.'

We walked on a bit further in silence, except the slap of that flat football bouncing against Danny's knees. Then he said, 'Can I come and watch?'

'Sorry, it's an away match, and there's not enough transport. As it is, Stockwell has to do two trips. Maybe next week, when we're at home.'

11
Playing away

Away games are scarier than home games.

First you meet at school and wait for Stockwell.

He chugs up in his van and takes the first lot. Then he comes back for the rest.

And all the time you're hanging about.

It's worse if you're on the first trip, 'cos then you've got to hang about at the strange school, and that makes you even more nervous. Strange buildings, strange paths, strange signs, strange people, strange smells. You feel like a trespasser.

School kit is special.

Or, it should be.

Stockwell comes into the changing-room and slams the big kit-bag down on the floor and rips open the zips. There it is, all the mess of kit, fresh from the launderette (I know he does it at the launderette 'cos we've seen him, on a Sunday evening), and everyone dives in and gets a shirt and shorts and socks. I always wear number 10. Bobby wears 6. Pete's number 9. And so on.

Our kit's yellow. Stockwell calls it 'gold'. But, I'm telling you, it's yellow. And blue shorts. It's old kit, it's cheap. It's not shiny and sleek with different stripes and flashes. It's plain old yellow, and itchy collars. The shorts don't all match. There's a scrum to get shorts that do match, and with good elastic. Most of the socks have shrunk, so the heel of the sock doesn't come as far as your own heel. Which is really uncomfortable.

But, it's still the school kit.

It's still special.

It still gives you a shiver inside when you put it on.

'Cos when you put it on it means Match Day.

In a strange changing-room, we whisper.

You can hear the other team shouting and singing and laughing down the corridor. They sound very sure of themselves. Confident.

We go outside. It's grey with a hint of damp. Threatening. Stockwell calls us round and squats down in the middle of the semicircle and gives us his pep talk.

'OK,' Stockwell goes, 'I know we've lost six games

in a row, but there's a long way to go. The league's not a sprint, it's a marathon.'

'This is the cup,' says Mitch.

'I know that,' snarls Stockwell, 'and that gives us an even better chance. In the cup, league form goes out the window. It's a one off. I know Northolt are a strong team, but it's only eleven against eleven. On paper they're by far the stronger team, but the game isn't played on paper –'

'It's played on the pitch,' we all shout.

Blah blah blah. He always says the same things.

'Remember, lads, if you want it enough, you can do it.'

I had a look round our team.

You've got to love them, but they don't give you a great feeling of confidence. They don't look like a team hungry for victory.

There's Mitch, our keeper. He's good, but recently he's lost it. Interest. He told Stockwell he didn't want to play any more, but Stockwell said he had to 'cos we haven't got anyone else to be in goal. Mitch is the only boy in our year who can grow a proper moustache. He greases his hair, and he's going out with Julie Devonshire. She stands by the goal while we're playing and chats to him, hugs herself to keep warm.

There's Moose, our centre back. Already one metre eighty, and bony. Forwards are scared of him, till they realise he's a big pussy-cat and he's slow and he can't really head the ball. If the ball's in the air, he makes sure he never quite gets there. Never meets it full on. If the ball comes near him on the floor, he hacks it as hard as he can and then chases after it like a cavalry charge. Apart from that, he's sound.

Then there's right back Kenny, who is little, but with big elbows. He runs like a whippet with his head down and his elbows pumping, and whoever's running near him is bound to get an accidental knock. Kenny isn't scared of anyone – the bigger they come the better he likes it, and he does like a scrap.

Bobby's right midfield. He's the vice-captain. He was captain in the first year, but then Stockwell made me captain.

Since then, Bobby's never liked me.

Bobby's a good player. He's short and he's quick, but he loses his temper over anything. As soon as things go the least bit wrong, his head goes down and he scowls and shouts at everyone and blames everyone but himself.

Especially me.

When he's in that kind of mood, he actually enjoys losing. The worse it gets, the better he likes it.

And up front we've got Pete. Pete is very pale and pink with gingery hair, and tall, not as tall as Moose, but he can head the ball. He's also very lazy and his hobby is smoking. Once in the league he pretended he was injured so he could go and have a fag in the changing hut. We were lining up for a corner and Bobby said, 'Look,' and there was all this smoke blowing out of the hut window. Everyone creased up. Except me. I was mad. But Stockwell didn't see, 'cos he was totally absorbed in the game.

That's the backbone of our team. The spine. We've also got Giffy and Moxy at the back and Andy P and Paul B in midfield and Johnny G is Pete's strike partner and on the bench we've got Chas and Stuart B and Jim. And there's me, I'm the captain, central midfield, and I'm not that quick but I've got a good engine, Mr Stockwell says. I keep running all day, and I can pass, and I can read the game. So Mr Stockwell tells everyone to give the ball to me, so I can pick out the best person to pass it to. I suppose you'd call me a play-maker. And I hate losing. And I never give up.

That's me.

It's Saturday afternoon, it's freezing cold, the ground is hard and rutted and the sky's getting darker by the minute. Stockwell jumps up from his haunches and says, 'Go and play football!'

12
Shaun

Moxy shivers, says, 'We haven't got a chance.'

'We have if Stockwell's ref,' said Mitch.

'Cos Stockwell, he cheats for us when he's reffing. They all do it, the teachers. Normally, they do one half each. So it evens out.

We know Northolt very well.

We've already lost to them once, in the league.

They come trotting out of the changing hut. They have this really slick kit: red and white squares with big numbers in yellow, and yellow shorts with trim, and red and yellow socks. They've even got a sponsor's name on the chest, 'cos one of the dads runs a company and he paid for the kit.

Their team trot out, passing these gleaming white balls one to the other.

They look so neat and grown up. Like men.

Shaun, their captain, comes over to me, stretches out his hand.

'Chris,' he says, 'so, you're still captain, eh?'

'So far as I know.'

And off he goes, flipping a ball from foot to foot, then exploding into a sudden sprint, head down, knees pumping.

Shaun and me go back a long way.

We went to the same junior school. He was head boy, school football captain, milk monitor, you name it. Everyone looked up to him.

He had this beautiful singing voice. He sang Joseph in the Nativity, with his arm round Mary, and I thought, what a sissy, but all of a sudden it was cool singing like Joseph with a high voice, and everyone was copying him and trying to get their arm round a girl to be Mary.

He was the best footballer in the school.

I was second best.

I was good at football but I had to work at it. I wasn't natural like him. He could do keepsy-upsy for two hours, telling jokes at the same time. He was always cool, Shaun.

I tried to copy him.

Never try too hard. Laid back.

We were captains when we picked teams, but my team always lost. No matter how close I got to beating him, he always found a way to win in the end.

When we were eleven he went to Northolt and I went to Kingsley. Since then, every year we've played each other twice, home and away, and every time, every game, they've beaten us.

Last year, in the away game, we came ever so close. We were 2–1 up with ten minutes left, but they won 4–2. Shaun scored a hat trick. He had a broken wrist. He played with it in a sling.

This year, in the league, we lost 3–0, away.

We've still got to play them last game of the season, in the return.

They have quite a lot of spectators, Northolt. Parents and girls and teachers and keener boys. Northolt, it's a real keener school. They're really into league tables and success. They know they're going to win.

This one dad, in a cap, calls out to Shaun, 'How many are you going to score today, then?'

Shaun shrugs, and smiles and trots over for the toss.

Oh, how I would love to beat him, and them, and see that parent bloke's face afterwards!

13
Northolt, game one

Right from the start of the game, they seemed to have more players than us. They were bigger, older, calmer, tougher. When they passed the ball, it went with a solid clunk off their boot and rolled straight and true to the feet of another player. Clean, sharp, quick.

They had so much time.

We were like flies buzzing round, lucky to get a toe in, lucky to belt the ball away for a few seconds' relief. Our passes were ugly, aimless. There was never anyone in space to pass to. If you got the ball, the Northolt guys were just swarming all over you.

When we took a throw in, our guys were brushed off the ball and Northolt got it.

When they took a throw in, there was always two or three of their players spare, open and moving forward.

Their penalty area seemed like it was miles away.

We couldn't make any progress, except hacking the ball and chasing. And then they dealt with it calmly, efficiently, shepherding the ball back to their keeper or letting it run out for a goal kick.

And the few times we got near their area, it felt like the enemy's impregnable fortress: dangerous, full of guards and bad magic and dragons. A scary place with cruel, calm, big blokes ready to take you out and hack you down.

At the other end, our area felt loose, vulnerable, open, up for grabs.

But, we did pretty well for the first half. They had all the possession, all the chances, but they only scored once. Stockwell was ref. I suppose he kept us in it with free kicks and off sides.

At half-time, his eyes were blazing.

'You're doing really well, lads,' he told us. 'I'm proud of you. If you can just hang in there and hit them on the break.'

But, once their ref took over, it was a different story. Their ref was much younger than Stockwell. He wore motorcycle boots, for some reason. He had little glasses and tight curly hair. He had a girly little mouth and he spoke very clipped, very precise.

We called him Angel Mouth.

Just after half-time, one of their midfield got a knock. Well, what I mean is, I kicked him. He went down like a sack of spuds, but the ref didn't blow up, so we played on. But this kiddy's still writhing on the ground, so Pete kicks the ball out. So their kiddy can have attention.

Which he got.

And we're lining up expecting them to throw the ball back to us, like you do. And Shaun, who takes the throw, he does throw it towards our goal, down the line, and Mitch is trotting out to get it. Except, their dodgy little winger, he comes darting across field, intercepts the ball, runs round Mitch, who is standing stock-still, and taps it into the empty net.

They're celebrating, the crowd is clapping and cheering, we're like totally puzzled, stunned, and Stockwell comes racing out on to the pitch shouting the odds.

'That's unsportsmanlike conduct, that is never a goal, you can't allow that, it's totally against the spirit of the game.'

Etcetera, etcetera.

Their crowd start booing him, and slow hand-clapping. And their ref, Angel Mouth, he's still got his little smile on his face and he's listening patiently, but all the time he's doing little shakes of the head. And when Stockwell finally quietens down, Angel Mouth says, 'I'm sorry, but no law of the game was broken, therefore I have no choice but to allow the goal to stand.'

Stockwell walks off, shaking his head.

That's why you've got to love him, even if he is a bit of a divvy. Because, he feels what we feel. He lives it, every kick.

They scored again, within a minute. I suppose we were still in shock, and after that it was embarrassing. But I don't think their ref cheated much from then on. He didn't have to. He just gave the right decisions. We did the rest ourselves.

Our defence went missing.

There was like an open corridor straight to our goal, with our players acting as guides on the way and a welcoming party when they got there.

I went back to help out, and Mitch played OK, but we'd lost all our heart. Every time they scored, I tried to get our team together and gee them up and make them work harder. Stem the tide. Damage limitation.

But it didn't work.

'Come on, Bobby,' I said, 'you haven't had a touch for ten minutes.'

He snarls back, 'Don't try and blame it on me.'

'I'm not, but we've all got to pull together.'

'You're not doing any better.'

And five minutes later, when I was in trouble on the edge of our box, and I was shouting, 'Give me some help, give me some help!' no one did help. Bobby was just standing there on the other side of the area. I had two men-on hounding me and the back pass to Mitch was cut off, so I tried to play it across the edge of the area to Bobby. And he could have got it, but he didn't even try. He just stood there, waiting for the ball. And Shaun intercepted it and took it in round Mitch and tapped it into the net for his hat trick.

And Bobby's there snarling, 'That was rubbish, Chris, you just gave that away.'

And so on.

Even Stockwell gave up.

After twenty minutes of the second half, he just stood at the halfway line, with his hands behind his back at attention, like he was waiting for the firing squad to shoot him.

Their supporters loved it. They laughed and cheered and clapped. And the worst part was, there was a sort of tone to it, especially from the parents, like they were sorry for us.

The final score was 9–0.

'Hard luck!' Angel Mouth said to Stockwell, shaking his hand.

Stockwell was nearly bursting with rage.

'Well played,' he said.

In the van on the way back there was dead silence. No songs, no chat, no nothing. I was sprawled on the big old kit-bag. It was dirty, squashed, flat.

'It's funny,' said Andy P in his loud voice. 'I don't feel like I've played in a game.'

Stockwell glanced back over his shoulder and snapped, 'You didn't, sonny, you didn't.'

When I got home, the doorbell rang.

Danny.

'Did you win?'

'No.'

'Did you score?'

'No.'

'Do training now?'

I explained that I was tired now but I said we'd do training tomorrow, definite.

Danny said, 'I can do keepsy-upsy now.'

To prove it, he dropped his big flat football down on his foot. The ball hit his foot and rolled away into the flower beds.

'One,' he said.

14
Dri-i-i-i-i-i-ing

Next morning was a beautiful morning. I knew as soon as I woke up. The blue sky and the yellow light glowing outside the curtains.

I jumped out of bed, looked out.

The phone rang.

I leapt down the stairs three at a time.

It was Pete.

'Coming down the park?'

'Course.'

Sunday!

Yes!

Perfect.

That's got to be the best feeling in the world, knowing you're going to get to play football all morning down the park, and no Stockwell or itchy shirts to worry about.

I couldn't wait – I was already gulping down some cereal, when –

Dri-i-i-i-i-ing.

My mum shouts, 'It's Danny!'

My heart sank halfway down my stomach. I'd forgotten him. And I'd promised him. Training. I was trying to think. I opened the front door.

Danny was standing like a statue at attention with slumped shoulders. He had his football with no air in it in the string bag. He was fully kitted out.

'OK, Danny,' I said, 'let's go.'

Outside, it felt even better than inside.

Blue sky, cold, slightly damp, the grass is long, the ground is giving. It's the kind of day makes you feel good. Full of hope. The thing you want most in the world is to run over that grass, with the ball at your feet, and pass it, a clean crisp pass, and run on, and get the return, and dribble through the tackles and fire the ball into the goal.

It's a great feeling.

Except today, it's me and Danny.

We trotted across the park.

Danny ran with his no-air football in the string bag banging against his fat legs.

I called, 'Why do you bring that thing? It's no good.'

'My mum,' he puffs back, 'she gave it to me.'

'It's ancient.'

'It was my dad's.'

We got to the swing park. The pitch where we play is round the next line of trees.

'Hang on,' I said. 'Let's do it here.'

We put our jumpers down.

We did passing, and shooting, and some tackling.

It was OK.

Danny was slow, but he got his foot on the ball more often than not.

'That's great,' I shouted, 'you're doing fine.'

The littlies came by. They shouted and laughed at us.

You could hear Bobby and Pete and the rest over the other side of the trees. Voices floating in the morning air. Laughter. The smack of boot on ball. I was thinking, if I can get rid of Danny in a minute, I'll still get a chance to play with the others for an hour.

Danny and me, we tried penalties.

I went in goal. Danny took the penalties from about four metres out. I made the goal as big as possible. I was willing him to score. But he couldn't. If he hit it hard, he hit it wide, or high. If he hit it straight, it was weedy. But, I would not let one in on purpose.

'If you want to score, you've got to score properly,' I shouted.

But Danny wasn't listening. He was looking behind me. Staring. I turned round to see what he was staring at.

15
BJ and a moped

About ten metres away, watching us, was a little knot of kids. In the front was Andy Stewart. With him, BJ. And Alex Fraser.

They're not in kit.

They don't play football.

They wear big parkas and baggy trousers.

They hang about, and smoke, and sometimes they ride bikes. At this moment, they're pushing an old moped. But, they've stopped to look at us. They're looking at us like we're a couple of nutters.

BJ walks over.

My stomach goes fizzy.

BJ is short and dark and walks with a swagger, and his parka is huge. He looks at Danny, looks at me.

'I didn't know you two were best mates.'

'They're not,' calls Alex Fraser, 'they're in love.'

They all snigger.

'We live next door,' I said. My throat was dry.

'Next door to what?' asks Andy.

'Each other,' I said.

BJ takes a little slap at the ball I'm holding.

'Come on,' he says, 'let's have a game.'

And with his other hand he knocks the ball out of my hand, and it rolls away, and he dances after it.

I didn't say anything. I know what they're like.

Andy and Alex chase after BJ. He tries to do a trick thing with the inside of his heel. It doesn't work. Alex hacks the ball clear. BJ grabs Alex's parka and pulls him over. Andy trips BJ from behind. They all three end up in a heap, wrestling and laughing and squawking.

The ball, they've completely forgotten. Danny picks it up.

BJ gets up, brushing himself off. Alex gets up too. They're both pointing at Andy and laughing. Andy is holding his ear.

And that's the kind of football they play.

It doesn't last long.

They push the moped off across the grass towards the trees. They're whistling, yodelling, shouting. Little high shouts, like yippee.

Danny watched them go.

Danny said, 'Why did you let them have the ball?'

'Because if you argue with them, then they'll take it and burst it or throw it out into the road or something. If you leave them, they get tired of it really quick. That's what they're like.'

Danny said, 'I'm not tired.'

'OK.'

So we did some more headers and tackles and passing. But, all the time, I could feel Andy Stewart and BJ and Alex watching, and I could tell what they were thinking.

I thought they might come back.

I thought Bobby or Pete or someone might come past. I felt guilty.

I picked up my jumper.

'Play a game now?' Danny asked.

'No,' I said, 'let's go home.'

Once we got out of the park, I felt better.

I dropped Danny off back home and then I sprinted back to the park.

But I was too late.

When I got to the pitches, there was no one there.

16
Secret

Next day, walking to school, Danny was skipping and scuffing along. He said, 'Can I play on the Block today?'

I looked at him.

'No,' I said, 'not yet.'

When we got to school, Pete asked me, 'Where were you yesterday?'

'Yeah,' said Andy P, 'we waited but you never turned up.'

'Something came up.'

'I reckon it was better without him, anyway,' Kenny said.

'That's right,' said Moxy, 'I reckon Chris is chicken. He knows Bobby should be captain.'

Bobby didn't say anything.

He was doing keepsy-upsy with a tennis-ball.

Danny was sitting on the wall, dangling his feet.

My secret.

Andy P had this theory about the thrashing we took against Northolt. He reckons it was down to the kit.

'They had such cool shirts and everything matching, and our stuff's such rubbish.'

'Yeah, that's right,' I said.

Danny and me, we did training in his sideway every day after school.

Every day, Danny asked, 'Can I play on the Block tomorrow?'

And every day I said, 'Not yet.'

He wanted to play in the C game on Thursday, but I wouldn't let him.

'You can't expect to improve overnight,' I told him. 'That'd be the worst thing you could do, is play too early. It'll undo all the good work we've done, and shatter your confidence.'

So, come Thursday, Danny was back with his black bag, picking up litter.

Me, Pete and Andy P had to play for the reserves.

It was Stockwell's idea.

What he said was, maybe the reason we're doing so bad this season is we don't get tough enough practice against the reserves on Thursdays. So, if we split the team, it'd make it much better training.

But Kenny and Moxy and Bobby, they were cock-a-hoop.

'You've been dropped!' Kenny said.

'It's 'cos you're no good!' Moxy said.

And it was a funny feeling, lining up with all the rubbish players, and no red bib. And no matter what Stockwell said, this thought kept niggling: OK, split the team, but why not let me stay with the bib and make Bobby play with the stiffs?

It wasn't a very good game.

I was in two minds.

One part of me wanted to go flat out and prove how good I was and how rubbish Bobby was. But another part of me said, if you try too hard and you lose, you're going to look really stupid.

So, in the end, I strolled it. I tried to look cool and superior, trotting round, slotting passes, never raising sweat.

I paid for it.

There was a fifty-fifty ball, me and Kenny. I thought I was going to get there easily. I took it too easy. Kenny threw himself in, 110 per cent. We clattered, kicking at each other, but he wanted it more. Before I'd really sussed it, he came away with the ball. I scrambled back.

Now I was pumped up. I wanted to take him out.

He's bustling along, elbows flying. I lunged in. He caught me in the ribs with an elbow. The ball ran loose.

I tried to get a foot on it but I slipped. Bobby danced in, flicked the ball away from me and slapped it into the net.

'Goal!'

There, on the touchline, is Danny, black bag at his feet, hands above his head, clapping.

After the game, Stockwell took me to one side.

'That was diabolical,' he said. 'You didn't even try. Don't you ever let me see you play like that again. It's not like you.'

I didn't say anything.

I thought he was probably right.

Walking home, Danny said, 'Aren't you in the team any more?'

I said, 'Of course I'm in the team.'

And next day, when Stockwell put the sheets up in the gym corridor, I was still in the team.

I was still captain.

After school, Pete said, 'Are you coming down the park tonight?'

I said, 'I might.'

Bobby chips in, 'He won't. He never does any more.'

'Some captain,' Kenny says. 'We're better off without him.'

Mitch says, 'Well, if Chris isn't playing, I don't think I'll bother either.'

I turned on him. 'Don't start blaming me 'cos you're going out with Julie Devonshire.'

He turns back on me. 'Well, that's a better excuse than you. What are you doing that's so important?'

Then I walked home with Danny.

'Training down the park?' he said.

'The thing is,' (I just thought of this) 'the main thing isn't what training you do with me, it's what you do on your own. All I can do is show you the basics, it's up to you to practise them.'

'What, like kicking and passing?'

He kicked at the damp air.

'That's right,' I said. 'You can do it in the sideway. Pass it at the wall, so it comes back to you. See how many times you can do it.'

Danny nods. Turns. Lumbers off round the little path at the front of the house. The bushes tug at him. He doesn't notice.

I went indoors.

Listening.

Sure enough. Five minutes later. *Thwack, thwack, thwack.*

That old airless ball, pounding against his kitchen wall.

I slipped out, to the park. Bobby was there, and Pete and Andy P and a few others. We played till it got dark. It was OK. I felt better.

When I got home, Dad was doing his stamps. He looked up.

'What on earth is that noise?' he said.

I listened. *Thwack, thwack, thwack.* Danny, still at it.

'Training,' I said.

If you listened hard enough, you could hear Danny counting – counting the number of passes he made without the ball getting off the wall and past him.

But he doesn't count in numbers. He counts in grunts, in his throat.

'Grr, grr, grr, grr grr –'

I was tired and I just wanted to sit and watch telly.

But that noise, it kept on and on.

Thwack, grrr, thwack, grrr, thwack, grrr.

After twenty minutes, I pulled my trainers on and a jumper. I went out the back door and round the side of the house. It was chilly. A moth was hurling itself at the bare bulb. Danny didn't see me at first. He's talking to himself. 'Chris to Danny.' *Thump.* 'Danny shoots.' *Thump.* 'Goal!' He throws his hands up.

'Nice one,' I said.

17
Draw

Next day was Saturday, and we played Fishbourne, and we drew 1–1. I played flat out, tried my hardest, covered every blade of grass. Bobby scored our goal. He hit it from about thirty metres, and it flew in. Everyone said what a great goal it was. We were happy in the showers, singing.

'See you down the park tomorrow?' Pete asked me.

'Try and keep me away.'

When I got home, my mum said, '*He* came round, again.'

I didn't need to ask who.

'What did he want?'

'What does Danny always want? Football, football, football. It's driving me mad.'

I went round to see him.

He was cleaning his boots. Picking the mud out of the seams with one of his mum's hairpins.

'How goes it?' I asked, cheerful.

He turned and looked at me. He was frowning.

'You said I could come to the game.'

'Did I?'

'You said it was a home game this week.'

'That's right. I forgot.'

'Did you win?'

'No, but we drew, and we played OK.'

'Did you score a goal?'

'No. Bobby did. Do you want to do some training?'

He nods and gets up.

He wanted to go to the park. I said, 'It's late, let's play in the sideway.'

I was in a good mood.

I was laughing and joking and urging him on.

I thought he was getting better and better.

When we finished, I said, 'I really think you are making big steps forward, Dan.'

'So, when can I play in a game?'

'Soon,' I said, 'soon.'

18
'What is that?'

Next morning, it was a beautiful day.

I still felt confident about Danny playing but I thought, not today. Probably next week. No point in rushing it.

I got up early, wolfed my breakfast and set off early for the park.

I ran round the trees, and there is the pitch.

The chalk lines are gleaming in the sun. The dew is glistening.

It makes your heart surge up your chest.

Most of the kids were already there, kicking about. It's not just Kingsley kids. Kids from other schools come and play. Sometimes you get older kids too, and younger. We play on the proper pitch they use on Saturday afternoons, except there aren't any posts. They keep the posts and nets in the changing huts and just put them up for the proper game.

But, it's still a proper pitch.

Everyone's up for it.

Bobby and Kenny, even Mitch.

'I thought you were meeting Julie,' I said.

'Yeah, well,' he goes. 'We changed that to this afternoon.'

Rows are forgotten.

Today is a new day.

We got started.

There's no tension. It's just pure pleasure. You still play to win, and play hard, but there's hardly any fouling. If there is a foul, there's no arguing. Everyone knows if it's a foul or not. You don't need a ref.

And you can show off a bit. You don't only think about clearing the ball or trying to score. You can do a few tricks like keepsy-upsy or back flicks.

I'd just scored a peach of a goal when I heard this kid called Ben shout out, 'What is *that*?'

I looked where he was pointing. There, standing by the side of the pitch, with his ball under his arm, is Danny.

'It's Blowsir!' Bobby shouted.

'What shirt is that?'

'Looks like Newcastle's old one.'

Ben said, 'Do you think it wants to play?'

I said, 'Leave him alone, he can watch if he likes, can't he?'

Kenny said, 'I didn't know you and Danny were best friends.'

'We're not friends,' I said. 'He lives next door.'

So Danny watched.

He stood with his ball hanging behind his back, with his whole face frowning. Peering out from under his eyebrows.

All the time, I knew he was there. It was like having a pet you've got to look after, but not so cute. You think he's going to run on to the pitch, or run away, or do something stupid. Or someone's going to say something to him.

The ball went out for a throw.

Bobby shouted, 'Come on, Danny, fetch!'

Danny dropped his string bag and lolloped off after the ball. Picked it up in both hands and tried to hurl it. It went behind him.

Everyone laughed.

'We've got ourselves a ball-boy,' Moxy said.

And next time he cleared the ball, instead of just

tapping it over the line, Moxy took a huge hack at it and sent it flying miles towards the trees.

'Go on, ball-boy,' he shouted, 'fetch!'

And off Danny went.

'That's stupid,' I said to Moxy.

'Stup-id!' he mimics back.

Danny puffed back with the ball.

Now everyone got the idea.

If they're over Danny's side of the field, when they kick it out, they kick it as far as they can. In fact, some people start belting it out of play when there's no reason.

Just for the hell of it.

Just to make Danny run.

Moxy kicked it right into the trees.

Off Danny went.

'Play properly!' I said.

'Play prope-rly!' Moxy mimicked back.

Danny puffed back with the ball. When he got near the pitch, he dropped the ball, and then stopped.

He stared at the ball.

Everyone is bawling at him.

'Come on,' Andy P shouts. 'Get on with it.'

Danny aims his shoulder at the ball.

He tippy-toes up to the ball and kicks it.

The ball scuffs off sideways.

There's a big tut from Andy P.

Mitch shouts, 'Come on.'

Pete shouts, 'Stop messing about.'

'Throw it.'

Danny chases the ball.

Andy P gets there first, pushes Danny out of the way.

Bobby and Kenny and Moxy, they're dancing round, waving their arms with limp wrists and doing stupid weedy kicks.

'That's not funny,' I shouted.

'Look,' shouts Johnny G.

There's this whining engine noise like a lawnmower bouncing.

BJ's riding this old moped out from the trees. Andy Stewart's hanging on the back.

Kenny and Bobby cheer them on.

Mitch and Moose, they flop down, picking at grass.

'Get off the pitch,' I shout.

BJ drives the moped in little swoopy circles towards us. He's got a sneaky face, like he's always making excuses for something. Nearly tips over, trying to balance in front of me.

'It's a public park,' he goes.

'Play on!' goes Andy Stewart in a silly voice, and blows a big whistle with his fingers.

So, we played on. Playing round the moped.

Andy S cheering and laughing at us.

BJ honking the horn.

The next time the ball got kicked away, Danny went after it, as usual. BJ fires up the moped and goes wobbling after Danny. Danny doesn't know. He's bending to pick the ball up. There's a sputter of engine, and a skid and mud flying, and BJ comes sliding along straight in front of Danny and kicks the ball away with his foot.

Everyone laughs and cheers.

Not 'cos it's funny.

To keep in with BJ and his mates.

BJ came wobbling back, dribbling the ball along with one foot.

'That was dangerous,' I said. 'You could have hurt him.'

BJ stops the bike and gives me a funny look.

'No wonder you're standing up for Fat Boy,' he says. 'He's your boyfriend.'

Bobby and Kenny go, 'Whoooo-hooo.'

But no one else does.

BJ says, 'They're always out together.'

Pete says to me.

'What's he on about, Chris?'

I shrugged, shook my head. 'Let's get on with it.'

BJ revs his bike, shouts out, 'Chris and Fat Boy, they were here, together, in the bushes, last week. Wa-hey!'

Everyone's getting interested.

BJ revved the moped, and spun away.

'Lover boys!'

'What's he talking about, Chris?' Moxy asked.

Everyone's looking at me.

Except Danny. He's got the ball at his feet, and he's trying to do flick-ups with his toe. It's not working too well.

I said, 'I've been doing some training with Danny.'

'Why?'

'So he can score a goal.'

Bobby haw-hawed. 'He already scored a goal. For Miss Gilbey. Against that table!'

Everyone laughed.

I said, 'A proper goal.'

'In a goal with posts and a net!' Moxy shouted in a silly voice.

'Well,' said Kenny, 'what are we waiting for?'

'Yeah,' said Moxy, 'if he's so good, let him play now.'

Danny looks to me, his face stretched, like it's up to me to decide life or death.

Bobby says, 'If he's got such a great trainer, he should be a world-beater.'

'OK,' I said, 'if you want him to play, let him play.'

19
Dannibrate

My stomach was fizzing.

I knew it wouldn't work. But I had to make it work.

We changed the sides round. Everyone kept arguing. Nobody wanted to be on Danny's side.

In the end, I said, 'Me and Danny, and Andy P and Pete and Mitch, against the rest.'

Andy P squawked at that.

'That's not fair, it's five against eight.'

'Who cares?' I said, 'let's just get on with it.'

We did.

I warned Bobby and his team. I said, 'Remember, Danny's only learning, so take it easy on him.'

'Yes, oh master of the universe,' said Kenny. And spat on the ground.

'Don't do that,' said Mitch. 'I might have to dive in it.'

To Danny I said, 'Go up front and hang about near

their goal. Kick anything that moves.'

So, Danny stayed up front. He chased the ball when it went up that end. He chased anyone if they had the ball. Them or us.

It was funny, having Danny on the field. I was watching him, not the ball. All I wanted was for him to do OK. But it's different doing training and doing the real thing. Just like it was with the kiddy game last week. The ball passed him by, the game passed him by.

'You're doing OK,' I called to him.

'He's so incredibly bad, it's amazing,' said Bobby, laughing, shaking his head.

'Leave him alone,' I said.

'Leave him alone!' Kenny mimicked.

Danny got a touch. The ball ran loose to him, and he charged up to it with his tippy-toe sort of run, and took a fly hack and connected pretty well. The ball flew miles away.

'That's better!' I called.

'Better?' wails Pinner. 'That's dreadful.'

'That's better!' goes Bobby, trying to imitate me.

'That's better!' echo Kenny and Moxy.

They were winning about 10–3.

I didn't care what the score was.

I got the ball. I passed it towards Danny.

Danny watched the ball coming like it was a torpedo and he was a ship. The ball hit his feet and bounced away. He takes a step back so he can kick it.

Moxy slides in and takes the ball, and Danny's legs. Down he went.

Moxy got to his feet, grinning.

I chased up to him.

'I told you to lay off him.'

Moxy turns on me. 'What is this, a game or what?'

Everyone's getting hot under the collar.

Bobby races up, spitting fire, 'If he's going to play he's got to play. You can't lay down the law. You're nothing. Just 'cos you're captain at school.'

The next time Moxy got the ball, he didn't move towards our goal. He waited. Danny was charging towards him. Moxy waited, and waited, and when Danny got there, Moxy did a pretend fall over, and left the ball.

'Oh no, Danny makes a fantastic tackle and gets the ball,' he shouts.

Danny pushes the ball in front of him, lumbers after it.

Bobby comes dancing across to him and flings himself, slow motion, away from the ball.

'Oh no, Danny with his silky skills beats one man. Can he score?'

Ben, who's in goal for them, he comes dancing out from the goal like a ballerina, fluttering his hands, and skipping.

Danny took a swing at the ball. It scuffed away towards the goal, but wide. Ben flung himself in a slow-motion dive, up in the air and down, and he batted the ball with the back of his hand so it rolled backwards and between the jumpers.

Danny stood there. He didn't say anything.

There's a moment of silence, then Bobby shouts, 'Goal!'

'Goal!' shouts Kenny.

Danny's standing there like a statue.

'Goal!' goes Moxy in a grunty voice, and does a stupid kick.

'Goal!' goes Bobby again, and waves his arms like a nutcase.

They all start doing weedy kicks and stretchy faces and they all shout in grunty voices, 'Goal, goal, goal.'

'Let's Dannibrate!' Bobby shouts, and suddenly they're all piling in on to Danny, slapping him and punching him and rolling him on to the ground, and he's grunting with laughter and trying to shield himself, and they're kissing him and hugging him. And punching him. And laughing.

Andy P's shaking his head.

'That was never a goal,' he goes.

Danny's still under the pile, they're all over him, punching and slapping. He's wriggling and trying to protect himself.

'Leave him,' I snapped.

Kenny and Moxy rolled away. Bobby was still kneeling on Danny, slapping at his face. I slapped Bobby round the back of the head. He sprang round and slapped me on the cheek.

We were squared up. My face was burning. He was snarling. I remembered this fight we had in the first year, punching and scratching and rolling over and over in the playground.

I won that one.

Just.

I bawled, 'If you're not going to play properly, don't play at all.'

Bobby snarled back, 'It's not worth playing, with him here.'

'Yeah,' shouts Kenny, 'he's spoiling it.'

'You can't have it both ways,' added Moxy, from a safe distance.

'You know what to do, then,' I shouted.

'OK,' said Bobby, in his stupid, clever, grown-up, swaying his head way. 'If that's the way you want it.'

And he picked up his jumper and walked away.

Moxy and Kenny and Paul B and some of the others, they went and picked up their jumpers too, and walked off.

Pete said, 'What do we do now?'

'Play on,' I said. 'It'll be better without them.'

Danny sits up, rubbing his ear. I reached down, got one of his arms – I needed both of my hands to get a hold – and pulled him up.

And we played on.

20
Fetch that

Bobby and his mates didn't go home. They moved away about fifty metres, and they put their jumpers down again and they started playing.

So, we had two different matches going on next door to each other.

I tried to ignore them.

The ball ran past Danny. He hacked at it. It curled off sideways.

I asked Pete, 'Do you think he's any better?'

'Any better than what?'

'Any better than he used to be.'

'He's rubbish,' Andy P said, running past.

'He's pants, as pants as he ever was,' said Giffy.

That was a sinking feeling.

'He's making the right shapes,' Pete said. 'Trouble is, they're nowhere near the ball, if you know what I mean.'

I did know.

Danny got the ball again. Giffy was on him. Danny scuffed the ball past Giffy.

Giffy did a pretend tackle, then fell over.

'Don't mess about,' I shouted. 'Play properly.'

Giffy is sitting on his backside, shaking his head.

'How can I do a proper tackle, on him?'

'How's he going to learn?'

'Why does he have to learn?'

'He's spoiling everything.'

'OK, if that's how you feel.'

I picked the ball up, and I tossed it in the air and whacked it.

It flew straight into the trees.

'Fetch that,' I said. And I picked up my jumper.

'Come on, Danny.'

Danny followed me.

Johnny G shouted after me, 'Spoilsport!'

The others joined in:

'You're always spoiling everything.'

'You ruined it.'

'He's so rubbish!'

'It's not worth playing.'

I walked past Pete.

I looked at him.

He looked away.

Danny didn't want to come with me. He kept looking back over his shoulder towards the others. I was angry. Angry at them for messing about, but angry at Danny too for being there and spoiling things.

Just as we reached the park gates, I heard this big shout.

'Play pro-per-ly!'

I looked round. Kenny had his hands cupped round his mouth. He shouted again, 'Give him a chance!'

In a stupid voice.

Everyone was laughing.

The two games seemed to be drifting back together again.

On the way home, Danny said, 'Was I any better?'

I said, 'Yes.'

He said, 'I don't care if they laugh at me.'

'Well, I do.'

I was a bit snappy.

He thought for a minute. Then he said, 'You play if you want to. Don't worry about me.'

I turned on him. 'Don't you worry, I'll do what I want, I don't need your permission.'

That evening, it was still light at seven, and it was mild and you could hear birds singing, but I didn't go down the park.

And, I didn't go training with Danny.

I sat indoors and watched the telly.

I hated it. I was squirming inside. I wanted to get out, to get away, to do something. But, instead, I just sat there.

And next door, I could hear it.

Over and over again.

Thwack, thwack, thwack.

My dad said, 'That noise is really starting to get on my nerves.'

'Same here,' I said.

21
The Block

I couldn't sleep that night, thinking about the park and BJ and Danny and Bobby. But I thought I worked it out.

Walking into school next day, I said to Danny, 'I think it's time you played on Thursday again.'

His face lit up. 'I'm ready?'

'Yes, because, I know you did OK down the park, but that was with the top players, you know, the school team, so you're bound to be out of your depth a bit. But, if you play in the C game on Thursday, it's more your level. I'm sure you'll do fine.'

When we got to school, I saw Johnny G kicking his tennis-ball against a wall.

'To me,' I shouted.

He kicked the ball the other way, to Kenny.

At dinner-time, we went out on the Block. That's where we play footie. The Block is the tarmac area stretching from the main road on one side (with a high wire fence), to the sports field at the other. Down the sides are prefab classrooms. It's a huge pitch. It must be about sixty metres long and sixty metres wide.

We play as many people a side as want to play. So, some days it's thirty a side.

And the pitch isn't just for football, or just for us. There are other kids there, chatting and playing other games too. You'd be rushing along chasing someone, and try and tackle them, and you go ploughing through some girls. And you might have another soccer match with kids from another year playing across the pitch the other way. It's crazy.

The rules are pretty strange. The goals are the whole fence at one end and the whole edge of the sports field at the other. Like rugby. And no goalkeepers. And the teams got picked to start with but, as the year went on, you knew which team you were in, and that was that.

We play with an old bald tennis-ball. Which is not easy. It bounces and flies, and you get it stuck under your feet. Everyone just goes howling after it. You can kick it miles up in the air.

Once Heather Field went to Mr Stockwell to

complain. And he was very sympathetic. To us. He suggested the girls stay round the corner in the small playground with the first years.

The Block is where Danny used to tear his trousers, getting tripped up and pushed over.

The Block is why his mum banned him from playing at school.

He sits and watches.

Today, he doesn't sit. He stands up. Watching the ball like a cat watching a bird, as if he wants to pounce on it.

Moxy shouts, points. 'It's super sub. Who wants him?'

Kenny joined in. 'He's in special training.'

'Here, Danny, what are you training for?'

'Show us your silky skills, man.'

I said, 'Leave him alone, let's play.'

'It's the trainer!' shouted Kenny.

'What did you teach him? To score penalties against Heather Field?'

I said, 'You'll see. You'll see what he can do on Thursday.'

Moxy got the tennis-ball. Put it down on the ground by Danny.

'Why wait till Thursday? Show us what you're made of, Danny.'

Danny kicked the ball. It dribbled off sideways.

They all cheered and laughed.

Kenny fetched the ball, brought it back.

Danny kicked it again.

I said, 'Are we playing or not?'

Johnny G turned on me.

'Come on, Chris, lighten up. It's only a bit of fun.'

'No one's going to hurt him.'

'Let him play.'

So Danny played, on the Block.

22
Danny plays on

'OK,' I told him. 'You're on my side. Stay close to me and you'll be OK.'

Danny stayed close to me. I stayed close to him.

The tennis-ball was a big problem for him. It was too quick, too bouncy. Maybe that was a good thing. He never got near it. If it got near him, he had no idea how to control it. But it meant he didn't get tackled.

He just ran about, got hot.

Heather and the girls sat and watched.

'Come on, Danny!' they're shouting.

I made Danny take all our kick-offs. Paul B got a bit shirty, but I told him, 'Cool it. What does it matter?'

Some kicks Danny scuffed, some he hit pretty hard. A couple of times Bobby or Kenny or Moxy did stretchy face and weedy kicks, but it didn't catch on.

The girls shouted at them, 'Leave him alone.'

I shouted at them, 'Get on with it.'

Alex Fraser and BJ wandered by and they did weedy kicks too.

'At least he's better than you,' the girls shouted.

The game seemed to last for ever.

I didn't enjoy it much.

I was always looking to see where Danny was.

But no one messed with him.

Until Pete scored for us. The ball hit the fence (which is the goal) and bounced away, and Danny saw it and his eyes lit up, and he charged up to the ball and whacked it, and it flew off sideways.

Bobby trapped it and set off down the pitch.

'Hang on!' we're shouting. 'It's a goal, Pete scored.'

'No,' goes Bobby, 'it's no goal.'

'Why not?'

'Danny played on!'

We had a big row. We said, a goal is a goal, you can't play on after a goal.

Bobby said, it's like playing advantage.

I said, what more advantage can you have than a goal?

But Andy P said, 'Bobby's right, Danny shouldn't have kicked it. That's like kicking the ball away.'

And then it all got confused, 'cos no one knows the

proper rules. And Mitch is shouting get on with it, and Moxy's mumbling and grumbling about Danny spoiling it.

In the end they said it was no goal.

So we played on.

And the next time we scored, Bobby picked the ball up, ran over to Danny and tagged him with it.

'No goal,' he said, 'Danny played on!'

That was enough for me.

I said, that's it, I'm not playing any more.

I walked off.

23
Chris 4 Danny

I walked round the corner of the science block. It's called the nature trail. It's quiet. You can throw stones at the old pig bins. They clang if you hit them.

Heather Field and some of the girls walked past.

'Sulking, are we, Chris?' she says.

I threw a stone at the pig bins. Missed.

'I don't like stupid games,' I said.

'Football's stupid, full stop,' Naomi Welsh said.

Then, Danny came trudging round the corner.

He had mud and muck all up one side of his shirt and trousers. I tensed up inside.

'What happened?' I asked. 'Was it Bobby?'

He shook his head.

'I crawled,' he said. 'Under the classroom. To get the ball.'

Danny sat down. About ten metres away. He was frowning. Listening.

From round the corner, you could hear the game on the Block.

Danny said, 'Why aren't you playing?'

I said, 'Because they won't play properly. They're just making fun.'

There was a big howl of laughter, some shouting.

Danny started, leaned forward, listening even harder.

'If you want to go and play with them, go,' I said.

Danny hunched over. Shook his head, like a shudder.

The girls walked past again. Naomi said, 'Oh, there's two of you now.'

'On a date, are we?'

I got up and walked round the corner, round to the back entrance. I pretended to be waiting for someone, looking at my watch.

The girls walked past again.

I looked the other way.

Round the corner, comes Danny.

The girls giggle.

I turned on Danny.

'Do you have to keep following me everywhere?'

After that, he kept his distance.

But, he still followed me.

On the science block wall, someone had chalked:

CHRIS 4 DANNY

Next day, I went to join in the game on the Block. Bobby and Kenny ran away waving their hands, shouting, 'Run for it, it's lurgy'.

'They're just being stupid,' Andy P said. 'Don't take any notice.'

'Don't worry, I won't.'

But I didn't play footie on the Block the rest of that week. I kept out the way. But it was hard, thinking of cool things to do. Especially with Danny hanging around. But Heather and the girls, they were OK. They said it was a good idea, training Danny up.

In fact, Heather found this old spongy rubber ball.

'You can do training here.'

I said no. 'It's no good here on the steps.'

'You're just embarrassed,' Heather said.

'No I'm not.'

'Prove it.'

So Danny and I did passing with this soggy wet old rubber ball with the rubber peeling off in bits. People watched. I felt like a fool. Half-hearted. BJ shouted something. Danny knew it wasn't right. He didn't charge about. He dabbed at the ball. Trying to be cool, like me. We must have looked really stupid.

Bobby came along. Brought Moxy and Kenny with him. Stood and watched with a snarly smile on his face. After a bit, he did pretend biting his fingernails and sang out, 'Aaagh. My place in the team is under threat.'

Then they walked off, laughing.

I didn't go down the park in the evenings, either. I spent the time with Danny in the sideway. Honing his skills.

24
Bagpipes

On Thursday, Danny brought his kit to school. In a red-check cotton bag like a table cloth with elastic drawstrings.

He was frowny, but excited. Nervous. Jumpy.

I'd not seen him like that before.

On the way to school, I gave him a pep talk.

'Remember, don't take any notice of what anyone says, and if they laugh, just keep playing, and do your best. That's all anyone can do.'

Danny nods, nods, nods.

'Don't let me down,' I said to him.

That made him frown.

All dinner-time, he sat in the cloakroom hugging his kit-bag, waiting.

After dinner, we went over to the changing hut.

Stockwell saw Danny and called over to him. 'Where's your broom, then, Danny?'

Danny stops still, frozen. Can't speak.

I said, 'He's come to play.'

'What's in the bag, then, bagpipes?'

'No, sir, it's his kit.'

Stockwell raised his eyes to heaven.

'What have I done to deserve this? We've been through all this once.'

I said, 'This time it's different. He's been training.'

'And who's been training him?'

'I have.'

'Right,' said Stockwell, 'I'll know who to blame.'

So Danny slips into the changing-room, furtive, like a hunted animal.

'Hey,' Alex Fraser shouts, 'it's Blowsir!'

'No,' says Bobby, 'it's bagpipes!'

BJ did a grunty noise.

Moxy did a stupid scuffy kick.

I didn't say anything.

Danny couldn't find anywhere to sit.

Every time he tried to hang his bag on a peg, the person next door threw a shirt over the spare peg.

We ended up in the extra bit right down the end by the sinks.

Danny was very slow getting changed. He takes

his socks off one by one, and then folds them, one by one. He folds everything neatly.

I went outside. Waited.

My stomach was full of butterflies.

I listened, to hear what they were saying in the hut.

'Superstar!' someone shouts.

'Blowsir!' shouts someone else.

Danny came out, blinking.

Heather Field walked past on her way to the netball court (Stockwell doesn't let the girls play football. He says they'll get too dirty, and they never remember their towels).

'Good luck, Danny, you can do it,' she called.

He went bright red and looked away at a litter bin.

Stockwell put Danny in the C game again. Of course. With the blue skittles for goals.

They kicked off.

The ball went one way.

Danny went chasing after it.

The ball went somewhere else.

Danny chased over there, too.

The weedy kids got out of his way.

Stockwell shouted over to me, 'If you're so interested in the C game, you can go and play in it.'

Danny chased a ball.

He barged past Stanley Farnsworth.

He got the ball!

But once he had it, it was like he was balancing on a barrel. His feet were all over the place. He looked one way, looked the other. The ball got caught up in his feet. Someone kicked it away.

Danny chased after it.

'That was better, surely?' I said to Pete.

'If you say so.'

Danny barged Billy Peters out of the way and hacked the ball high in the air.

'Look,' I said, 'he's getting into it now.'

'That's right,' said Mitch.

'He's footballer of the year,' said Pete.

Our game got started.

I couldn't concentrate.

It was like part of me was out on the C-game pitch.

It felt as if it was only me being there, watching, that was keeping Danny in the game. The fact was, Danny was worse now after all our training than he had been before. Because, before, he just charged about. But now, he had all these things to think about that I'd taught him. So he had to think before he ran. And he tried to form his body into the right shapes. So it was more like someone posing for a photo than trying to play football.

'Danny, get stuck in!' I shouted.

'Chrissy! Concentrate!' shouts Stockwell.

That's when it happened.

25
Dazzer

What I think happened was this: BJ was standing like he does with his hands in his pockets, dreaming of his post-match fag, but the ball ran near him. Danny went tearing after the ball and went straight through BJ, and knocked him over. BJ may be small, but he is hard. No one messes with BJ. So, he makes a big deal of it and turkeys up to Danny, and Danny won't back off, 'cos he doesn't understand about backing off, so BJ has to punch him.

That's when the shouting started.

And we all ran over.

BJ was hitting Danny. Danny didn't fight back. Danny didn't go down. Danny didn't run away. That's what he's like. So BJ had to go on hitting him. Otherwise he'd lose face. So he's pummelling Danny, not very hard, and Danny's standing his ground, blinking and ducking and putting his arms up.

I ran over, I got between them.

BJ stopped pummelling. I think he was glad someone got there. He turned on me. BJ, he's never liked me. He didn't say anything, he just punched me. I've not been punched for ages. Right on the nose. It hurts like a sting with bits flaring up into your eyes. Not a bad hurt. It makes you angry.

I swung back at him. Hit him on the shoulder. Weedy.

He swung back at me, harder, and this one landed on my ear, so everything went boomy like underwater, and I staggered sideways and I fell over.

BJ spat down on the ground beside me.

Then, Danny went ape. He went for BJ like a storm. No science, no plan. The only way I can describe it is, he ran him over. He bulldozed him. And he got all over him, and then he held him. And all the time, BJ's squealing and hitting Danny.

But Danny isn't taking any notice. Danny's got him down, and he's holding him down.

Finally, Stockwell arrived. You can't move fast in galoshes.

'Danny, let go of him, we don't have fighting here,' he said.

From underneath Danny, BJ piped up, 'It's not fighting, sir, it's a misunderstanding.'

That brought the house down.

'Come on, Dan,' I said, 'let him up.'

Danny let him go.

BJ scrabbled to his feet.

Danny gets up. He's so clumsy getting up, you can see Stockwell wincing.

Danny asks me, 'Are you all right?'

'Yes, of course I'm all right.'

Andy Stewart had to put his oar in, 'It spoils it, Danny playing. He doesn't know what he's doing.'

'Well,' said Stockwell, 'he may not know what he's doing, but at least he's trying.'

'He's still rubbish,' whispers Bobby.

Everyone laughs.

'Right, then, Danny,' says Stockwell, 'I think from now on you'd better go in goal.'

Stockwell turns to all the other no-hopers, 'And if anyone so much as touches him, they'll have me to deal with.'

So Danny plays on.

He doesn't know much about goalkeeping. He fell over a lot and grazed his knee. He let five or six goals in. He gave it everything. The ball hit him here, hit him there. He did manage to connect with one clearance. He caught it so clean, it flew off sideways right over the hedge and into the road.

After that, no one said anything. No one made fun of Danny. And no one went anywhere near him. It was very polite.

Me, I had another terrible afternoon. This week Bobby played for the reserves, and so did Kenny and Moxy and Johnny G, and it ended up 3–2 to them. For their second goal, I passed the ball straight to Johnny G by mistake.

'Wake up, Chrissy,' shouted Stockwell.

At the end of the afternoon, when we were all trooping off from the kickabout, Stockwell trotted over to Danny, slapped him on the back and said, 'Well played, Danny.'

And Bobby calls out, 'His name's not Danny, sir, it's Dazzer.'

I slapped Danny on the back and said, 'Well done, you did it.' Danny was out of breath, and smiling and frowning at the same time.

In the changing hut, everyone called him Dazzer. It was good. They were all talking about his tackle on BJ.

'That's what comes of having Chris as a trainer,' Pete said.

They all laughed and cheered. I felt good. I felt like I'd done it. Maybe he was still rubbish, but at least he'd made his mark. And it took the pressure off me. If it wasn't for him, everyone would have been laughing at my mistake in the main game.

'Cos Danny's so slow changing, we were the last ones in there. I was bubbling on about how well he'd done, and he must be proud.

He stopped pulling his sock on, and looked at me, and said, 'There's only one thing.'

'What's that?'

'How can I score a goal if I'm in goal?'

'Well,' I said, 'you won't always be in goal. And it is a start.'

'Can I play in the real game next week?'

I swallowed hard. 'That's not up to me, that's up to Stockwell.'

'Oh, right.'

'What you've got to do is keep trying, and show him you're up for it.'

'You think I can do it?'

'Yes,' I lied. 'I'm sure you can if you keep trying.'

'Good,' he smiled, and pulled the sock all the way on. It was a long, very long, sock, which his mum made him wear to keep his calves warm.

All the way home he was darting backwards and forwards, pretending to kick long balls into the box, or nodding flick ons. He did some pretend saves, too.

It was my turn to be quiet. Because, though the game had gone OK, seeing Danny in action, I had this feeling he was never ever going to get good enough to play in a proper game.

Let alone score a goal.

26
Notice-board

Next day, I was on edge.

Andy P spread this rumour that Stockwell was thinking of making changes in the team.

Moxy said I was going to get dropped.

At dinner-time, I wandered round the school, trying to keep away from people I knew. I could hear the Block game howling away in the distance.

At ten past one, I went round through the small playground. The girls and the little kids playing their stupid games. The older girls standing and sitting in huddles.

Heather Field shouts out, 'Fancy some skipping?'

'No thanks, not today,' I shouted back.

I kept on walking. Strolling. Casual.

I knew where I was going.

Round the boiler-house corner.

The gym.

You're not allowed indoors at dinner-time. Not unless you've got a cold or an excuse.

They put monitors on patrol at all the doors.

So you can't get in.

So you have to stay outside.

I slipped in the boiler-room door.

It's a grey door with slats and writing in big red letters: AUTHORISED PERSONNEL ONLY.

I slip along the boiler-house corridor.

It's hot and smells of coal.

The air's all steamy.

The boiler-house corridor runs up to a double door. Through that you come out through another slatted door in the gym corridor.

I walked along briskly, with my head up, like I was on a special mission. Which I was. The gym corridor was empty, except for Mrs Drew walking along with some papers. She's a secretary. She looked at me a bit funny, but she doesn't know anything about rules and stuff. She clattered on past.

I got as far as the notice-board. Stopped.

Standing right next to the notice-board, staring straight at it, was Danny.

The teams were up.

Danny was standing right up close, with his head over on one side to read. Carefully squinting at each name in turn. He turned round and said, 'I'm not in the team.'

I didn't know what to say.

I had my own worries.

I went up to the board.

I didn't look at the top of the list, I looked lower down, and then across, and then up. I was holding my breath. It was like an electric shock. My name wasn't there, it wasn't there. My eyes keep flicking.

Then I saw it.

Right at the top of the sheet, my name, 'Captain', with a gap under it so it didn't look like I was part of the team.

Then the others all came swarming in. Jostling and pushing and peering over each other's shoulders to look.

Pushing Danny out the way.

'What's he want here?' laughed Moxy.

'He thinks he's in the team,' said Kenny.

'I'm afraid you didn't quite make it, Dan,' goes Bobby.

'Not even reserve for the no-hopers,' goes Moxy.

'Dazzer, still the king of rubbish!' says Bobby.

'So much for training,' goes Kenny.

Danny turned away from the board. Everyone's laughing and joking.

'Never mind,' I said.

Danny nodded. His mouth was puckered up, like he'd really been expecting to be in the team.

After school, outside the classroom, waiting for Danny, Pete said to me, 'I don't know why you encourage him. You're only making things tough for yourself.'

'And for Danny,' Mitch added.

I said, 'I wish I could stop but what can I say to him? He's so thick he doesn't realise just how bad he is. He's worse than bad – I mean, yeah, I wish I'd never started it.'

The door opened. Danny came out.

'Hi,' I said.

We walked home in silence. He didn't run, he didn't growl, he didn't scuff at stones.

27
No fun

That evening, I was sitting in my bedroom.

I had that sleepy end-of-the-week, glad-I'm-home feeling. I was aching a bit and I had a bit of a sniffle in my nose. I was playing this football game I invented. You play it on your own. You use chess pieces and a chessboard and a dice. I played all the league teams in the Premiership, one on one, so you got a proper league table. It went on for ages. I didn't tell anyone else about this game. Not my parents, especially not my friends. If my friends came round, I hid the book I kept the results in.

Mind you, I hadn't had any friends round for a couple of weeks.

I was playing this game and I was trying to relax but something was bothering me. I couldn't work out what it was, but then I twigged.

It was quiet in the sideway next door.

No *thwack thwack thwack*.

I tried to finish Chelsea v Arsenal.

But I couldn't.

It was bugging me.

I went next door. Danny was in his bedroom, playing with his ancient computer game. It's just a dot that slides across the screen so slow you can't believe it. He's frowning with concentration.

'No training tonight, then?'

He doesn't look up. He's toggling his joystick trying to catch up with this slow-moving ball that's floating like a feather across the screen. The ball on his screen sinks into his goal. 4–0 the machine.

Now Danny looks up. His eyes are very serious, like he's been thinking about this for a long time.

'I don't want to do training.'

'Why not?'

'Because you don't want me to play.'

'It's not what I want, it's what you want.'

He glared at me from under his eyebrows.

'It's not fun any more.'

'Whoever said it had to be fun?'

'Everyone's still laughing at me.'

'Yes,' I said, 'not everyone, not out loud, but most

people they are still laughing at you.'

'They say I spoil it.'

'That's their problem.'

'That makes you cross with me.'

'I'm not cross with you.'

'Because they laugh at you too, now.'

That got to me. It riled me. I jabbed down the off button on his computer, and the screen sizzled blank like a pan of sausages.

'Look, Danny, if the others don't like it they can lump it, OK?'

I'm thinking, what are you saying? If Danny gives up, it's the best thing can happen. But something inside me won't let go.

'So,' I said, 'are you going to give up now or are you going to keep trying?'

'I'm never going to be good enough to get in the team.'

I said, 'OK, maybe you're not good enough yet to get picked, but there are other ways to get into a team, you know?'

'How?'

It just came to me. I remembered what I did when I was in the second year to get into the softball team,

135

even though I wasn't much good at it.

'You turn up for every game, and you bring your kit and your boots, and you make yourself useful, and sooner or later we'll be a man short, and you'll get a game and you can play. Even if it's only ten minutes as a sub. What do you say?'

28
Dead keen

Next day, I called for Danny. He was very sheepish.

'Where's your kit?' I asked.

He pointed to the corner of the kitchen where he kept it.

'Come on, then.'

He dragged over to his kit-bag, picked it up, and off we went.

It was an away game. At St Anthony's. Everyone was hanging about outside the gates. Waiting for Stockwell.

Danny kept his head down.

He was embarrassed, everyone looking at him.

Bobby piped up, 'What's he doing here?'

I said, 'He's with me, OK?'

'Why's he got his kit?'

'Just in case we're short, that's all,' I said.

'Well, we're not.'

'He's not doing any harm, is he?'

'He always spoils it,' Kenny said.

Stockwell drove up in his van.

I went up and asked Stockwell to have a word. We had several words. He said he picked the team, and Danny wasn't in it, and if every Tom, Dick and Harry who thought he ought to be in the team turned up, he'd have to hire a double-decker bus. I said, ah, but they don't turn up, do they? And you've got to make two trips anyway.

'And Danny's dead keen. He'll be useful for carrying the half-time oranges and packing the kit and stuff like that.'

Stockwell glanced at Danny.

'He doesn't look very keen.'

'He's just nervous.'

'OK, but you look after him.'

'Don't I always?'

'And, anyway,' said Stockwell, 'the way you've been playing recently, he'll be challenging for your place.'

29
Nightmare

When we finally got down to playing the game, I had a mare. I had one of those games where I was always in the wrong place at the wrong time, so I was stretching for balls or getting them caught under my feet, and no one seemed to be there to bail me out. Every time I tried to take someone on, they took the ball and left me for dead.

Within a couple of minutes, Bobby was snarling at me and then Kenny and Paul B and Moxy joined in. I was clumsy as a cart-horse, my feet kept getting stuck in the ground. It was a damp, wet, misty day, and I started going hot, and then hot and cold. Big waves of temperature running up so I blushed and then I shivered.

Danny stood on the touchline with Stockwell and the subs. Every time I lost the ball, Danny clapped his hands and cheered.

St Anthony's are the weakest team in the league,

including us. They never have a good team. I don't think their headmaster likes football. They can't run and they can't tackle and they don't even shout at each other.

I made another terrible mistake, for their first goal. I got caught with the ball on the edge of our box, and I tried a back pass but I scuffed it too short, and their striker nipped in and took it away from Mitch and scored.

'I don't know about you training Danny,' Andy P said. 'It's more like he's been training you.'

And Bobby scored our goal. He dribbled past two defenders and slotted it into the far corner. Almost before he'd finished celebrating, Moose scored. An own goal. With his head! That's the kind of season we're having.

So, come the second half, they were leading 2–1. Stockwell was on edge, shouting and bawling and pointing. One of their lot hoofed the ball out of play. It bounced along past Stockwell and Danny.

'Dazzer, don't just stand there,' Stockwell shouts. 'Make yourself useful. Fetch the ball.'

So Danny darts off after the ball and picks it up in both hands and lumbers back with it.

'Quickly quickly quickly, we're running out of time.'

Danny hurls the ball with all his power back to Giffy, throwing it so hard he nearly falls over himself.

Then we equalised, a nice goal. Bobby went down the wing, he skinned the full back and crossed for Pete. And Pete nodded it in from the six-yard line. 2–2.

'Concentrate!' Stockwell shouts. 'Keep your shape!'

Sure enough, they came back at us for the last few minutes. They had their best spell of the game. We were happy just to kick the ball away. Giffy hammered a beaut across the halfway line and way out towards some bushes near a fence.

Stockwell bawls from the touchline, 'Nice one, Giffy, keep it there.'

But, suddenly, puffing up beside him with the ball is Danny. He's really got into this ball-boy business, charging up and down the touchline. It's a job he can cope with and enjoy. He thinks he understands it.

'What's the rush?' snarls Stockwell.

Danny hurls the ball to their bloke and the throw comes in. The ball squirms through Moose's legs, Giffy stretches out a foot, misses, and their weediest bloke darts in and blasts it past Mitch into the roof of the net.

We've all got our heads in our hands.

Stockwell's got his head in his hands.

Danny's standing there with his hands above his head, clapping.

Then the final whistle goes.

We trudged off.

No one spoke to me.

No one spoke to Danny.

It was icy silence in the van on the way home.

Afterwards, after Stockwell dropped us back at school, I tried to explain to Danny about fetching the ball.

'You see, you didn't have to hurry so much. If you'd taken a couple of seconds more, it would have been time, and we'd have got a draw.'

'But Mr Stockwell, he told me to hurry.'

I took a deep breath.

'That was before, when we were losing. Once we scored the equaliser, we wanted to slow the game down, so they don't get a chance to get a winner.'

He thinks about that for a while, then looks at me.

'But that's cheating.'

30
First pick

Next morning, I went to the park.

I didn't feel like going. I had a bit of a sniffle and a headache, but I still went.

I made Danny come with me.

Johnny G took one look at Danny and said, 'Not him again.'

Paul B said, 'This is getting beyond a joke.'

Johnny G said, 'It's not worth playing.'

'It's a total waste of time,' Moxy said.

'Not if you want someone to tackle BJ,' Bobby said.

And that made everyone laugh.

'Let's pick sides,' I said.

'OK,' said Bobby.

He picked Danny first pick.

Everyone hooted.

I didn't say anything.

When I picked Johnny G, he wouldn't play with me.

'OK,' I said, and picked one of the no-hope hangers-on instead.

The game got off to a bad start, and it got worse.

I had a row with Mitch. He was in goal for us. He rolled the ball out to me when I was marked, and I lost the ball and Johnny G scored, 'cos Mitch didn't even try and save it.

'What's the point,' he said, 'if you keep giving the ball away?'

'You shouldn't have rolled it out to me.'

And so on.

Then Bobby had a shot from about ninety miles out, and Mitch just watched it go in.

I had another go at him. He pulled his gloves off and went. Just like that.

'I've got better things to do,' he said. 'It's supposed to be fun.'

So I went in goal. But Giffy, who was supposed to be fullback, instead of tackling out front, every time they attacked, he'd drop back behind me and try and save it on the line.

'I'm supposed to be in goal!' I yelled at him. 'Get out front and tackle.'

31
Goal

They were winning 15–2, or something like that.

Our heads were down. Bobby and his boys started taking the mickey. Passing backwards and forwards. Trying to make us chase. But Moose wouldn't chase. Or Paul B. He was lying on his side on the grass with his head on his hand.

'Come on, Dazzer!' says Bobby.

So Danny comes hippy-hopping along with the attack. Just me and Giffy left to beat. They're all coming for us, Kenny and Bobby and Moxy and Andy P all doing little three-centimetre passes between them.

And Danny's in the middle of it. They keep giving it to him. And he scuffs it off. And they fetch it and give it back to him. They're doing slow-motion running and Danny faces and weedy kicks.

Danny has got this huge grinning, giggling look on his face. He's yelping with laughter.

'Tackle him!' I shout to Giffy.

He goes out. Hunched over, one shoulder down.

Bobby goes, 'Last man to beat!' And does a slow-motion pass to Kenny. Who does a slow-motion run towards Giffy, then slips the ball to Danny.

'Tackle him!' I yell. 'Cos this is the chance to get the ball away.

But Giffy, instead of doing a proper tackle on Danny, he's caught the disease. He does a slow-motion tackle. Like a replay on telly. He swings in ever so slowly and, on purpose, he misses the ball completely and goes sprawling flat, and everyone laughs and they howl, 'Go on, Dazzer, put it in!'

Danny tips it with his toe. I know his style. I know what comes next. He's going to run at the ball and take a flying hack at it. I'm not going to give him the chance. I go belting out from the goal. Danny's hopping up to the ball. I go straight over the top of the ball, diving sideways, spread out, and I take him out. I flattened him. I rolled over on top of him. I dug my elbow in his chest, and I put my hand on his head and pushed his face into the mud as I got up.

Bobby and Kenny push me out the way. They're whooping. Moxy's doing a jet-plane dance.

They pull Danny up.

I look back behind me.

The ball's gone in the goal.

Danny scored, and I let it in.

'Let's Dannibrate!' shouts Moxy, and they're all diving in over Danny, slapping him and punching him and rolling him on the ground, and he's grunting with laughter and saying, 'Goal! Goal! Goal!'

Bobby's clutching his stomach, bent over, howling, 'You let it in. What a wally! You let it in!'

I bent down and picked up my jumper.

And I walked off.

When I got to the corner by the swing park, I looked back.

The Dannibration was still going on.

32
Get Well, Chris

Next morning my alarm went, but I didn't get up.

Danny rang the bell at half eight.

Mum shouted up the stairs.

I shouted back, I was ill.

I stayed in bed all day. By the evening I *was* ill. I had a headache and a sore throat.

Danny came that night. He had a yellow bruise on his cheek.

He gave me this card he'd made himself. Made out of grey sugar paper, with a crayon picture of a stickman in football gear. The writing said, 'Get Well, Chris.'

Inside, there were all these signatures, all the team, and Heather and the girls. He told me all about school. About how he'd been playing footie on the Block again. How it was really good.

'They call it Plays On,' he said.

I said, 'And, you scored a goal yesterday.'

He shook his head. 'That wasn't a proper goal.'

'Yes it was.'

'You let it in.'

'Not on purpose. I tried to save it.'

He shakes his head again.

'It still wasn't a proper goal.'

'Why not?'

'There was no net.'

33
Bobby captain, Chris friend

I stayed off ill right through to Friday.

I didn't feel totally OK by Friday but I had to go in to show Stockwell I was available for Saturday.

'Cos Saturday was home to Northolt, the last league game of the season.

I couldn't miss that.

Moxy sneered when he saw me. 'I don't know why you bothered to come back,' he said. 'You won't be in the team.'

'Yeah,' goes Kenny, 'Bobby's going to be captain.'

'Yesterday he scored a hat trick and Stockwell said, "that's more like it".'

I didn't answer. I pretended I didn't care.

Mitch still wasn't talking to me.

Pete said he didn't blame him.

There was a crazy mood all morning. People passing scraps of paper with their team selection on it.

More and more scraps of paper went round.

It was fun. Everyone was high, trying to pass as many pieces of paper as you could and not get caught. When you got one of the pieces, you had to scribble out the players you didn't like and scribble in the ones you did.

As the morning went on, my name was getting scribbled out an awful lot.

I didn't do any scribbling.

I just passed it on.

Kenny wrote 'BOBBY CAPTAIN' in huge letters on one sheet, so it covered the whole paper. That appealed. Soon there were all these sheets with BOBBY CAPTAIN in huge letters. Then someone put 'Chris Oranges' in tiny letters on one of the BOBBY CAPTAIN sheets. That brought the house down.

Moxy got this sheet with 'Chris captain' on it. He took a long look, shook his head, then screwed the sheet up. He did it loud, so Mr Enyon heard. And looked. But didn't say anything.

Soon all the sheets with me in the team got screwed up and there were just five or six BOBBY CAPTAIN sheets going round. Now the game was to think of something stupid to put about me in little letters.

Then, as soon as someone thought of something, it got passed to me.

BOBBY CAPTAIN, Chris rubbish.

BOBBY CAPTAIN, Chris go home.

BOBBY CAPTAIN, Chris kiss Heather.

They got stupider than that.

All lesson, Danny was sitting there watching the papers being passed. No one passed to him. It got to about five minutes left and Moxy collected all the sheets. He waited till Mr Enyon had his back turned, then he crouch-darted up the aisle, and plumped the pile of sheets on Danny's desk.

That appealed!

There's lots of sniggering and tight lips and snorty noises coming out of noses.

Danny looked at the top sheet.

Moxy hissed to him, 'Come on, you've got to write.'

Mr Enyon looked round. Danny was carefully writing on the top sheet. Mr Enyon strode over and snatched the sheet up. He frowned as he tried to understand what he read.

'Bobby captain?' he said.

There was a big cheer. Then silence. Tense. Was this one of the dirty ones?

'Chris – friend?'

That brought the house down. Roars of laughter. Roars of it.

When the bell went for the end of morning, Danny sat at his desk, looking very puzzled and serious.

'What's up, Dan?' I asked.

He looks at me. 'Do you like Bobby?'

I smiled. 'Of course I do. I love him to little pieces.'

A big smile spread over Danny's face. He slammed his desk lid down.

'Good,' he said. 'I like him too.'

And he was up, and away.

34
Dazzer Plays On

I went round by the nature trail.

I could hear the shouting and laughing from the Block.

It didn't sound like football.

It sounded like hunt-chase or something.

The shouting and laughing got louder and more stupid.

Andy P came by. He had his puzzled look, which he gets when the stats don't add up.

I asked him, 'Why aren't you playing?'

He sat down next to me. 'Because it's not like proper football.'

'What are they playing, then?'

'You don't want to know.'

Five minutes later, Mitch and Pete came past, shaking their heads.

Pete said, 'See what you started, Chris?'

I edged round to the wall by the main entrance so I could see the game. It took me ages to work out what the rules were.

It went like this: you had to score a goal, but that wasn't the main thing. No one tried to stop you from scoring a goal. You could hand ball it, throw it, anything. Once you'd scored the goal, everyone, but everyone rushes over to one of the prefab classrooms. They scrabble about under the classroom, where there's an old heavy flat football hidden.

This is the juicy risky bit of the game, 'cos it's against the rules. You're not allowed to have a real football in the playground, 'cos of the windows. If Stockwell sees you with a real football, you get jumped on from a great height.

Anyway, whoever gets there first gets this ball and then they chase after Danny. They don't have to chase much, 'cos he's run over to the prefab classroom as well. Then they have to throw the ball as hard as they can at Danny, and then everyone shouts, 'No goal! Danny played on! No goal! Danny played on.'

The harder you throw the ball at Danny the better, especially if you can hit him in the face.

Then you've got to hide the ball again under the classroom.

Danny, he doesn't give up. He doesn't complain. He doesn't cry. He's a bit puzzled but he keeps chasing with everyone else. In fact, he's smiling, giggling.

He's enjoying himself. And, there's a big rip in the leg of his trousers.

BJ's playing. So's Alex Fraser and Andy Stewart.

Alex Fraser throws the big ball and it hits Danny smack on the nose.

There's a little trickle of blood.

I ran over, grabbed the ball.

'It's not funny,' I said.

Bobby snarls back, 'It's none of your business.'

BJ says, 'What's your problem?'

'It's not funny,' I said again.

'What's not funny?' asks BJ, like he hasn't got a clue what I'm talking about.

'Throwing the ball at him.'

'It's a game.'

I couldn't speak. Any words that came into my head sounded stupid.

I turned to Danny.

'Come on. Let's go and get you washed up.'

He shakes his head. 'I'm playing.'

'But it's not a proper game.'

He sniffs and wipes at the blood with the back of his hand. He's scowling at me. I look him in the eye. He reaches out and snatches the ball away from me. And throws it to Bobby. Bobby catches it, turns to me.

'Is it OK if we play on? I wouldn't want to do anything to upset the captain.'

'Just because you're captain,' sneers Kenny, 'you think you're better than anyone else.'

Moxy pipes up, 'You won't be captain for long.'

'Yeah,' goes Paul Miller, 'Bobby, he should be captain.'

I turned round and walked off. As I walked off they all laughed. Except Danny. He chased after me, caught up.

'Don't you want to play?'

'It's OK,' I said. 'It's not my scene.'

I walked on.

I thought he might have followed me. But as I turned the corner by the gym, I heard them all laughing again, and the loudest laugh of all was Danny's.

35
Lift

At the end of dinner-time, there was a stampede down to the gym corridor. Everyone went howling down there. To look at the notice-board. Except me. I went back to the classroom. I looked out the window.

I saw Bobby come out of the main doors. Moxy and Kenny were walking backwards in front of him, gesturing with their hands. Bobby was shaking his head. Behind Bobby, lumbered Danny.

Pete came in.

'Well,' he said, 'you're still Stockwell's little darling.'

My heart stopped.

'I'm still in the team?'

'You're still captain.'

Bobby didn't let on he was upset.

'We'll see, we'll see,' he said. 'There's things we can do.'

Afternoon break, they didn't play football. Or Plays On. Bobby sat on the wall. All his mates crowded round him. And Danny was sat on the ground underneath him, and Bobby's got a tissue, and every now and then he tears a bit of paper off his tissue and sprinkles it down on Danny's head like snow. Danny feels it fall and brushes it off. And laughs.

After school, I waited for Danny.

Bobby and Moxy and Kenny walked past with Danny.

'It's OK,' Bobby said. 'My dad's going to give him a lift in the car.'

36
Mutiny

That night, I got a call from Andy P. He said he'd
heard a rumour that Bobby and Kenny and Moxy
weren't going to turn up for the game tomorrow.

I said, 'Thanks for telling me.'

'Shouldn't you tell Stockwell?'

'No,' I said, 'it's good riddance.'

Then I started thinking.

I started thinking, who have we got if they don't
turn up? Our subs are Jim and Chas and Stuart B.

OK.

What if *they* don't turn up?

And then I started going a bit hot and cold.

About half nine I rang Moxy.

'Are you playing tomorrow?'

'Maybe.'

'What's maybe about it?'

'Well,' goes Moxy, 'there's a lot of this flu going

about. You're not the only one that's allowed to have it.'

'It's the last game of the season.'

'It doesn't mean anything, does it? We can't win anything. And anyway, it's Northolt. We're bound to get hammered.'

I said, 'That's no reason for not turning up.'

'Are you begging?'

I put the phone down.

37
Sick

I didn't get much sleep that night.

Next morning, I called round for Danny.

'He's not here,' his mum said. 'He went out with some friends. Bobby, and Kenny?'

'Where did they go?'

'Swimming, I think.'

I got to school early.

Then I waited.

The boys started turning up.

Pete and Giffy and Moose.

'Hi,' I said.

Giffy said, 'You look lonely.'

Pete said, 'You look worried.'

So that's four.

Then Stockwell arrived with the kit-bag and Miss Gilbey.

'What's she doing here?' Giffy asked.

'Maybe she's come to play,' Pete said.

Stockwell thumped the kit down in the changing hut, came out.

'Where is everyone?' he said.

'They'll be here,' I said.

'Well,' said Stockwell, 'Mitch won't.'

'Why not?'

'He's got the flu. So, we need a keeper.'

I went icy.

'Since when did he have the flu?'

'His mum rang me this morning.'

Andy P and Johnny G arrived on their bikes.

Pete said, 'That's six.'

Andy P said to me, 'Any sign of Bobby?'

I shook my head.

I said, 'Can I borrow your bike?'

'Sure,' he said.

I got on, pedalled off.

At the gates, I passed Jim and Stuart B and Chas.

'Where are you going?' Jim shouted.

'Nowhere,' I shouted back. 'Just get changed. You're on. All of you.'

I rang Mitch's doorbell.

His mother opened the door.

'What is it?'

'Where's Mitch?'

'He's in bed.'

'Can I see him?'

She stepped back and I went in.

I ran up the stairs, pushed open his bedroom door.

He was huddled up under the covers.

'What the hell are you playing at?' I said.

'What does it look like?' he said. 'I'm sick.'

'Don't give me that. Just 'cos we had a row –'

I pulled the covers back.

He turned his head to look at me.

He was flat out. Pale. Crusted round his nose.

'OK,' I said.

'What's up?'

'Nothing. Only we're about ten men short.'

'What do you want me to do about it?' he croaked.

'Pray for us,' I said. And went.

38
Trophy

Back to school.

I thought, maybe by now Bobby and the others have turned up.

Outside the changing hut, Stockwell is fuming.

'What the hell's going on?' he says. 'We've got nine men and we're playing the league leaders.'

I went into the changing hut. The guys are sitting there like a bunch of lost sheep.

Andy P's going, 'I just don't understand it.'

'I do,' said Johnny G. 'Chris, he's put everybody's nose out of joint. No wonder they won't play. I've got a good mind not to play myself.'

'Don't then,' I snapped. I was trying to find the number 10 shirt in the kit-bag. There was an awful lot of shirts left to choose from.

Andy P's moaning on, 'How are we going to play Northolt with only nine men?'

The door slapped open.

I went icy.

I didn't dare look up.

'Make that ten,' goes Pete.

There, standing in the doorway, is Danny.

'Better get changed,' I said, 'looks like you're in.'

'Hooray,' goes Giffy, 'now everything's going to be all right.'

'He can't play,' said Johnny G.

'They'll laugh at us.'

I said, 'He plays.'

I went outside. Just in time to see Northolt arriving. They came in force.

Not just the usual Northolt five or six cars. There were ten or twelve cars and two minibuses full of kids. There was Angel Mouth, their ref with the motorcycle boots, and parents, and this other bloke, very stiff and solemn and dignified, shaking hands like he was important.

'Who's he?' I asked Pete.

'Search me.'

'I think it's their headmaster,' Andy P said.

Stockwell went and greeted them.

'Don't they look smug,' I said.

'They've got every right to be,' Pete said. 'They are the champions.'

'That's not quite true,' Andy P said. 'Not if we beat them.'

And he starts trying to explain the detailed stats.

Giffy shouts him down.

'Fat chance,' says Pete.

The Northolt team walk past us. They're smiling and chatting. They've got proper kit-bags slung over their shoulders. They look older than us, wiser, smarter, you name it. We're like beggars by the side of the road in our scruffy yellow shirts and shorts that fall down.

They march into the changing hut, laughing and shouting just like they're at home.

We kicked a ball about, waiting. The nerves were eating me. I felt like we were trespassing on our own field.

Then this huge black car pulled in.

We all stood and looked.

Out of it got this bloke in a sharp black suit.

The Northolt head and ref went over and shook his hand.

Stockwell went over, too, and hovered.

The Northolt games master said something to Stockwell.

Stockwell called me and Pete over.

'Go and get a table, will you?'

We ran over to the school building, got a table out of the hallway. I felt stupid, like a servant.

'What's it for?' I asked Pete.

'I'll give you three guesses,' he replied.

We set the table up in front of the big black car. The suit bloke went round to the back of his car, opened the hatchback and fetched out this huge gold thing.

'What is it?' Moose whispered.

'That's the league trophy.'

'What, for us?' said Moose.

'No, you idiot, for them. That bloke in the suit must be from the schools' league. He's going to present them with the trophy after they've seen to us.'

'That's why their headmaster's here,' said Chas, 'that's why there's so many people.'

My heart was pounding, my blood was boiling.

I turned to Andy P.

'Come on stato. What's the situation in the league?'

'If they beat us, they're champions. If they draw with us, they're still champions. If we win, and Ashley

Court beat Montrose, Ashley Court win the league.'

'I think I understand that,' I said. 'You realise what that means?'

Giffy said, 'We're rubbish and they're top of the table.'

'What it means,' I said, 'is that they are taking the mickey. Not just them, but the bloke with the suit. They're all assuming they're going to beat us. Like it's a foregone conclusion. Like it's not worth playing the game.'

'So?' said Johnny G. 'They are going to beat us.'

'They already beat us twice this year.'

'9–0 in the cup.'

I nearly exploded. I said, 'Football's a funny game. It's only a one off. If we want it enough, we can do it. After all, it's only eleven against eleven.'

Pete says, 'Not exactly, we've only got ten men.'

'What does it matter?' I said. 'If we really give it everything, we can give them the shock of their lives. Maybe we can't win that trophy ourselves, but what we can do is make it as hard as possible for them to win it.'

Andy P and Moose and Giffy are nodding.

Chas and Johnny G are shaking their heads.

'One other thing,' says Pete. 'Who's going in goal?'

That stopped me in my tracks.

And then this voice, behind me, 'I'll do that if you like.'

It's Mitch. Looking like death warmed up. Already changed, in his trackie.

'That's eleven,' I said.

'Except Dazzer,' says Andy P. 'Where's he got to?'

39
The smell of goals

Danny was still in the changing-room, huddled in the corner, where two anoraks are hanging, like he's trying to hide. I grabbed a shirt and shorts and two socks out of the bag, and took them over to him.

'Come on then, get changed.'

He takes the shirt, stares at it.

Number 11.

It's like he's frozen, pure white.

'Come on, Danny, it's what you wanted.'

He rubs the shirt against his face.

'You didn't call for me,' he said.

'I did. You were off with Bobby.'

'We went swimming,' he said.

'Was it fun?'

'They pushed me in.'

He looks up at me and then he farts. This big windy frightened fart like a scared animal.

'You'll be OK,' I said. But I tell you I was as nervous as hell, too. Your stomach goes tight and your throat, and all these eels are wiggling down there.

I had to go to the bog.

When I got back, Danny's sitting in the corner with his shirt on. And this look on his face, like he can't believe it's him.

'You look great,' I said.

The nerves went wriggling up and down my guts again, even though I'd only just been. My mouth was dry. I felt very irritable and nasty, like I could hardly bear to talk to him.

'Come on,' I said, 'it's time to kick off.'

He looked up. He had one of the practice balls in his arms, like a baby. He was crouched over it, sniffing it.

'What are you doing?'

He sniffs, looks up. 'Smelling the ball.'

'Why?'

' 'Cos it smells of goals.'

Andy P put his head round the door.

'Come on,' he said, 'they're ready to toss up.'

'Come on,' I said. 'We're late.'

Danny stood up, still cuddling the ball. Stood there.

Under the shirt, bare-bum naked. Sets off clattering for the door.

'Shorts!' I shouted. Picked them up off the floor. Waved them.

Danny trots back dutifully, like a dog.

I snapped at him, 'Can't you do anything right?'

And that does it for Danny. He's pulling these shorts on, getting his legs all mixed up, and he's crying, too.

That's the first time I ever saw him cry.

The only time.

I held his arm, for balance.

He got the shorts on.

They were loose, even on him.

I tied the string, in a bow.

'Keep one hand in your pocket,' I said, 'or you'll lose them.'

Carefully, he felt for the pocket.

There wasn't one.

'Come on,' I said.

40
Tactics

We ran out of the changing-room. It was a long way to the pitch. I could see Stockwell and the others, and the more we ran the further away they seemed to get, like a nightmare.

We had to run past the Northolt team.

They were chuntering about late kick-offs and maybe the game should be forfeited. They watched us all the way past.

'What is *that*?' one of them said.

And they all laughed. It felt like the whole world was looking and laughing. 'Cos I've got this Danny thing dragging along behind me, like they used to make criminals drag behind them in the Middle Ages, like clanking cans. It was as if I had my insides hanging out for everyone to see.

Stockwell's there in the centre circle with Shaun the Striker. Shaun, of course, is as cool as you like, arms

174

folded, foot tapping. Stockwell is on edge, keeps looking at his watch.

'I'm very sorry about this,' he says to Shaun, 'we've had a flu epidemic. But we'll try and give you a game.'

'I'm sure you will, sir,' says Shaun.

Smoothie!

Stockwell says, 'Call,' and flips the coin. My insides flipped up with it. Shaun called tails, tails it was. Then he offered me his hand again.

'May the best team win.'

'I hope not,' I managed to say, ' 'cos that'd be you.'

And then he was striding away. I felt like I was frozen inside myself like an ice cube in a fizzy drink.

Stockwell said, 'How many have we got?'

'Eleven, with Danny.'

'Danny?' His eyes lifted to heaven, then closed.

We trotted over to the rest of the team. Stockwell raps out his instructions.

'OK, we'll play three up front. Stuart, you go up there with Pete and Johnny G. Chas, if you cover for Kenny on the left and, Jim, if you go on the right.'

Stockwell takes a deep breath, turns to Danny, talks much slower. 'Danny, thanks very much for turning out. Congratulations on getting your first game for the school. I want you to play left midfield. Can you explain that to him, please, Chrissie? Then maybe we can finally get this game kicked off.'

He trotted away. To have a final check with Angel Mouth the motor boot.

Danny said to me, 'Where's left?'

'Don't worry about left.'

'Sir said.'

'Forget what sir said. I've got a special plan for you.'

And I had. It just came to me.

I said, 'Now look, we've found that if you try and chase the ball you never get it, do you?'

He nods.

'Well, then, it's obvious. What I want you to do, is try and get as far away from the ball as you can.'

Danny's already making faces. This is tough for him to understand. I try again.

'Wherever you see the ball, you run somewhere else.'

He nods. Still looks puzzled.

I'm thinking, if he's out the way, nothing bad can happen, can it?

'But stay onside!' Andy P says.

'What's that?' Danny says.

'Aaaah!' goes Johnny G.

Giffy's got his head in his hands.

'Never mind,' I said.

We never had got round to theory lesson two.

Stockwell blew his whistle. My insides went icy again.

'What are we doing?' Pete asked.

I said, 'We're going to fight and fight and fight and never give up and we're going to show them. We're going to rub their noses in it.'

Then I smiled.

'Just think of it, at the end of the game, if we've won and that bloke with his suit has to pack that trophy up again and stick it in the back of his car and take it to Ashley Court!'

That got through.

'I like it,' Mitch said, through a noseful of snot.

Another car pulled up by the field. This bloke got out with a big camera.

'The papers are here!' said Mitch.

'OK,' I said, 'let's give them a story.'

41
The sucker

Lining up for the kick with Danny on the field felt really weird. I had this horrible feeling about leaving Danny there on his own. It was like leaving a big bleeding stupid part of me out there for everyone to see and laugh at. Because I knew, now, I wished he hadn't come. Even though we were a man short. I knew he was going to make a fool of himself, and of me. I wanted to say to everyone – it's not my fault, I don't know him.

I hissed to Pete, 'Let's try the sucker.'

Pete grinned, shook his head. 'It never works.'

'So? What have we got to lose?'

From the kick-off, Pete touches the ball to Johnny G, he touches it straight back to me on the edge of the centre circle. Meanwhile, Pete and Johnny G are pelting forward as fast as they can. I whack the ball as high as I can, as hard as I can. The idea is, you do it so quick, you catch them off guard.

It never works, except this time. This time it worked.

Northolt weren't in any kind of shape. The ball fell between their two central defenders, Pete leaps up like a salmon and nods it sideways and Johnny G hits it first time from the edge of the box. Johnny G likes shooting from long range. He's got a powerful shot on him. But not very accurate. Nine times out of ten the ball flies up and wide and way offbeam. But this time, he caught it sweet as a nut, so it flew, lifting, towards the top corner.

I thought it was in, my mouth was already open, but their keeper threw himself and made a great save. But he couldn't hold it, and the ball bounced out and – yes! – there is Pete. Calm as you like. Like he's been standing there on the edge of the six-yard box all day waiting for a bus. Side-foots it past the sprawling keeper, into the far corner.

For a moment, there's dead silence.

We can't believe it.

They can't believe it.

The crowd can't believe it.

Even Stockwell can't believe it – but then he blows his whistle, a long, long, loud blast.

And there on the touchline is Miss Gilbey and Heather Field and Julie and a couple of younger kids, and they're jumping up and down and shouting.

There's Stockwell, pointing back to the centre. His eyes are wild. I think he was the most pumped up guy in the whole place at that moment. He was so excited he'd gone red and he was panting for breath. Trouble is, being ref, he can't show it. He hissed to me, 'That'll show the so-and-sos. Now, just keep it up and keep them out.'

We're all over the place. Johnny G and Pete, they've run back, arms round each other, and Andy P and Moose and the rest, they're climbing all over them, hugging and shouting and slapping each other and clenching fists.

I'm pulling them apart.

'Come on,' I said. 'Concentrate. Forget three at the front. Stuart, drop back in front of the back four. Johnny, come deeper, play sweeper. We're going to play defensive and we'll try and catch them on the break. Every chance you get, just pound it up field. Aim for Pete, to try and get his head on.'

'What about you?'

'I'll take care of Shaun.'

Northolt, they're standing around, all lined up for the kick off. A bit embarrassed, slightly impatient.

Shaun smiled and shook his head.

'Nice goal,' he said, 'make the most of it.'

'Don't worry,' I said, 'we will.'

42
One on one

I marked Shaun one on one.

I stuck to him like glue.

Everywhere he went, I followed him, and sometimes I got there first. He's quicker than me, but I wouldn't let him go. I pulled his shirt, I tugged his shorts, I got in his way, I pushed him, I blocked him, I tripped him.

Shaun's got his arms out, appealing to Stockwell. 'Come on, ref, give us some protection.'

Stockwell ignores him.

Northolt, first they were cocky, 'cos they thought our goal was a fluke and they couldn't help slaughtering us, and so they played slow, patient passing football. But every time they got into our final third, we hacked it away. Pete stayed up front on his own. He's so tall, and he's got good control. He held them up.

Mitch was white as a sheet. And, he had a shaky start, dropping a couple of crosses. But then he made a stonking save from a header and, after that, he got that look he sometimes gets.

'They shall not pass.'

Moose and Giffy, they were giving it the long boot every chance they got.

And Stuart, Chas and Jim, the new boys, they were playing out of their skins. I suppose they were fired up. Waiting to get in the team all season. They were everywhere, chasing, covering.

And if the ball did get through, through to the byline or through a hole in our defence, it was funny how Stockwell noticed some foul or other infringement, and blew his whistle and gave us a free kick.

This one time it was so blatant it was embarrassing. They'd pulled our defence over to the left. The cross came over, beat everyone except their number 10, who was about ten metres out. The ball bounced nicely. He went to smack it with his right foot, but Jim came burrowing in from behind like some small burrowing animal, all legs and arms. He took the number 10 out, and I think Jim hand-balled it as well.

Northolt all scream penalty. Stockwell blows his whistle. They all go, 'Yes!' But then Stockwell raises his arm and points down the other way.

'Indirect free kick for the Golds,' he goes. 'Obstruction.'

And Danny?

Well, after half an hour, he hadn't had a touch. Which I suppose means he was doing what I told him. Every now and then the ball went over him, or round him. But, he was doing a job. For the first half an hour, Northolt marked him. They shadowed him all round the pitch. Shouting to each other:

'Check the runner!'

'Watch 11!'

'Winger's coming through!'

Until the thirty-second minute.

I was on the halfway line. With Shaun. He's ducking this way, turning that way, and I'm sticking with him. He darts forward into our half.

I'm with him.

Their number 7's got the ball on the left.

Shaun makes his run.

Moose shouts, 'Move up.'

Our back four move up.

Johnny G moves up.

The number 7 hits the ball over the top, in front of Shaun. Who's clean through.

'Offside!'

I've got my arm up, Moose has got his arm up, we've all got our arms up.

But the whistle doesn't go.

Shaun is still running, chasing the ball.

Stockwell goes pounding past me.

Shaun is clean through, except for: Danny.

And I know what's happened.

Danny's on the edge of our box, because that's where he's run to get away from the ball. But by running there, he's played Shaun the Striker onside, who would have been offside if Danny hadn't wandered back behind our back four. And now Shaun the Striker is running straight at our goal, with just Danny and Mitch to beat.

'Tackle! Tackle! Take him out!' We're all shouting it, but I know it's hopeless. Shaun the Striker is running at pace with the ball tied to his foot, and Danny's standing there with his side-on look, crouched like he's waiting for someone to do a leapfrog over him. Mitch, he's trying to come out and narrow the angle, but Danny's there like a roadblock right in his way.

All Shaun's got to do is take it round Danny with two touches and stick it past Mitch, who's in two-man's land. Shaun does the first bit. He shows Danny the ball, Danny sticks out a leg, Shaun pulls the ball back the other way. Beautiful move, all in a split second, and Danny's leg's going one way and Shaun the Striker's going the other way with the ball. But here Danny's clumsiness comes into the equation. If Danny sticks a leg out one way, the equal and opposite reaction is, he falls over the other way, and sure enough over he goes like Bambi on ice, and he throws his arms out to save himself, and he ends up ooof with a thud and a stumble and a mess of arms and legs all over Shaun the Striker.

It looked like a rugby tackle.

Northolt, they're all shouting, 'Penalty!' and I clocked Stockwell. In my head I'm going, don't give it, don't give it, and I saw the look in Stockwell's face, the sneaky-ferret cheaty look, and I knew, he won't give that.

Their lot, the groan's gone up already, and I'm shouting, 'Clear it!'

But we can't. Mitch can't get the ball.

Because Danny's sat there on the ground and he's picked the ball up.

'What the hell are you doing!' bawls Mitch.

Danny looks up, surprised. 'I fouled him.'

Stockwell had to give the penalty.

He had no choice.

No one talks to Danny.

No one looks at him.

Andy P says, 'Just make sure there's no one in the area.'

We're very quiet.

Shaun comes up to take the kick. My mouth is dry. I walk past Mitch and whisper, 'He always hits it left.'

Mitch nods.

Shaun hits it right.

He hits it sweet and low.

Mitch goes right, too. The right way. Stretching, arching his back. Gets his fingers to it. The ball slithers against the post, then round it. Out for a corner.

Bedlam.

Everyone's slapping Mitch on the back, and Andy P slaps Danny on the back and says, 'Great tackle, Dazzer, you saved a goal!'

After that, Northolt forgot about Danny.

Someone shouted, 'Watch number 11.'

And their number 4, a short, stocky kid, he shouts back, 'Watch him yourself, he's not going anywhere.'

And so it got to half-time.

We were still 1–0 up.

43
Half-time

Stockwell ran off the pitch with me. He said, 'That's half the job done and it won't get any easier.'

No, not with Angel Mouth reffing.

'Why are you playing so deep?'

'I'm marking Shaun.'

'Damn right you are. If you get much closer you'll need a legal separation after the game. And what's Johnny G doing?'

'Playing sweeper.'

Stockwell nearly screams, holds it back.

'We don't play a sweeper.'

'We are today.'

'We play a flat back four. They're all over us.'

'They're the better team,' I said, 'but we're winning.'

He looks at me, narrowed eyes.

'OK,' he says, 'but watch it. You so much as touch

one of them in the box in the second half, and you
know what'll happen?'

I nodded.

I got the team in a huddle.

'That's great, guys, you're all playing out of your
skins. We can do it. We can do it.'

Andy P points over to the gates. 'Look who's
here.'

I look.

It's Bobby, Moxy and Kenny.

Johnny G shouts, 'Come on, Bobby, Kenny, get
changed, we're 1–0 up!'

'Hang about,' I said. 'So who comes off? Chas?
Stuart B? Jim?'

Johnny G looks puzzled.

I said, 'That was the best team performance over
forty-five minutes we've had all season. No bitching,
no heads going down, hundred per cent commitment.
Why should we change?'

Paul B goes, 'What about Dazzer?'

'Yes,' says Johnny G, 'he only gets in the way.'

'He's doing all right,' said Andy P.

'Yes,' I said. 'This is a team performance and
we're not going to break the team. Especially not for

the sake of one of those whingers. Dazzer plays on. Any objections?'

They all shook their heads.

Bobby came over. Sheepish.

'Hi,' he said. 'I'm feeling better.'

'Good,' I said, 'keep wrapped up warm.'

44
Number 4

The second half started.

For a while, they stayed patient.

We kept chasing, blocking, tackling and hacking the ball away.

I stayed with Shaun.

My throat was burning and my legs felt like Plasticene, but I stayed with him.

Moose kicked one out for a throw.

I had my hands on my knees, panting.

'Kick it further next time,' I shouted.

Their ref trotted past and looked at his watch.

Very obviously.

As though he was totting up every wasted second.

They started to get some free kicks.

Mitch made a great save from close range after a corner. A few minutes later, he charged out and sprawled at the feet of their number 10, who was through. Smothered the ball.

Their number 8 hit the bar.

It was one of those games.

They were all over us, but they couldn't score.

And, the longer it went on without them scoring, the more frustrated and careless and desperate they got, and the more their crowd started muttering and jeering and shouting, 'Come on Northolt!' like you would to a naughty dog.

And the more we began to work together like a team. We actually got some possession, and played triangles. So they had to chase us, chase the ball.

The tackles started flying in. If we tackled, it was a free kick to them, if they tackled, it was play on, even if our guy is down on the ground with blood flowing.

They got another free kick, on the edge of our area.

I was in the wall with Moose and Giffy. Shaun belted it. I flinched. Moose didn't. He stretched his neck and the ball hit him splat in the face. It made a wet smacking sound. Down he went. But the ball was away. Giffy hacked it clear. Again.

I pulled Moose up.

'That's the way,' I hissed. 'Keep doing it.'

'There's a first time for everything,' panted Giffy.

Twenty minutes to go. I was getting pumped up inside. I was actually starting to believe we could do it. So was the bloke with the suit and the trophy. He's looking at his watch, feeling his collar. Uncomfortable.

They attacked again. We were all back except Pete. Chasing and hounding. Andy P ran back thirty metres, slid in, cleared the ball.

'I'm dead,' he shouted. He could hardly breathe.

Nor could I. My throat was on fire.

'Keep going,' I shouted back. 'Last ten.'

I told Pete to come back now.

'It's all hands to the pump.'

Even Danny showed up in our area.

'Get away, get up there,' I shouted at him.

Off he went again.

'And stay away from the ball!' I yelled.

They kept pressing. It was never ending. Every time you cleared, it went straight to one of their blokes. And came back again. But we kept our shape, kept covering. You get into a sort of trance, sliding in, falling over, running back, covering the angles, marking the runners.

And the more chances they got, the more snatchy they got.

'Come on, Northolt!' shouts one of their dads. 'This is pathetic.'

The ball went left, back to the right. Their wide man skinned Chas. The cross comes over, hanging. I jumped, it grazed the top of my head, flew back, hit Shaun in the chest, bounced off. Dropped on the six-yard line. Their number 10 was there. But Giffy sprawled in and on one knee he hacked the ball behind for a corner.

'Come on,' I shouted. 'Don't let up.'

The corner came over, Mitch went out and claimed it. A big jump. Safe in his arms wrapped to his chest. Except their centre back number 4 had come up, and he went in like a double-decker bus. Caught Mitch in mid-air. Knocked him flying. The ball spilled out.

No whistle.

'Play on!' their ref's shouting. 'No foul!'

Shaun's darting in. I got there first, levered the ball across out of the area to Stuart B. He tries to play it forward to Paul B on the edge of our area! The ball sticks in the mud. Their number 5's in there. He hacks it, it hits Moose, and Giffy whacks it out for a throw.

I'm screaming at Stuart B, at everyone, 'Keep it simple, just knock it up the other end.'

Mitch is still down, flat on his back.

I went over.

'Are you OK?'

He nods. 'Winded. I didn't even see him coming. Who was it?'

'It's OK,' I said. 'I've got his number.'

We were getting pushed further and further back.

'You're too deep!' Stockwell bellowed. 'Push up.'

But we couldn't. We were exhausted, and they were all over us. They were all pushing up. Their number 4 had the ball, moving in on our area.

There was Danny, in front of him.

The number 4 starts taunting him.

'Come on, Superstar, tackle, go on.'

Danny tackled him.

Well, what he did was swing his leg and hack the number 4 on the shin. He didn't mean it.

The ball ran away and Giffy hacked it clear.

The number 4 is rolling on the ground, looking for a free kick. Angel Mouth the ref is already running back up the field, shaking his head.

So the number 4 gets up, like he's suddenly right as rain, and he punches Danny twat in the mouth. Ref didn't see. No whistle.

By now the ball's coming back. The number 4 trots away. Smirking.

'I saw that,' I said.

'That nutter,' he says. 'Shouldn't be playing.'

The ball comes through to him, on the edge of the box. He's so cocky, the way he's standing there like he's got all the time in the world, rolling it under his boot.

I left Shaun, and went for the number 4. He didn't see me coming. I got him with my elbow and my knee and I landed on his face.

Whistle.

Free kick, on the edge of the box.

As I got up, I hissed in the number 4's ear, 'Leave the nutter alone or you'll get afters.'

The ref had a yellow card out. He made me turn round, to get my number, like it was a proper game.

I didn't care.

I was running round like a maniac, urging everyone on, saying all the stupid things you'd never say if you weren't pumped up: 'Come on, Giffy, we can do it. Keep it tight, Chas.'

The free kick came over, floated. There's ten of them and ten of us go up for it. The ball drops, everyone's hacking. Like pinball. Their fullback whacks it – thud. It hits Mitch, rolls out. Shaun darts in, hits it again, and I thought, no, it's in, but Mitch is up again and throws himself the other way and blocks it with his body. He's grovelling along the ground trying to grab it but he can't, and then we're all in there like a scrum, hacking and kicking, and no one can get a clean kick at it. The ball's scuffing round inside the six-yard box.

Until Giffy manages to hoist it with one of his big boots, and the ball goes sailing like a lame duck, up in the air and away.

I ran up to the ref.

'How long?' I gasped.

'That's my business,' he says.

'It's time!' shouts Stockwell. 'Game over! Blow your whistle!'

45
That beautiful ball

The ref didn't blow.

Back come Northolt, their number 10 gets round Johnny G but Jim and Stuart B are there sliding in, and somehow they get it back up to the halfway line. Andy P chases up, and he chases their blokes all along the halfway line. He never gets near the ball, but he keeps them occupied, making them pass sideways.

They play the ball up, and in. I slip, Shaun shoots, Mitch palms it round for a corner. Again.

Poor old Andy P, he's standing with his hands on his knees on halfway, having a blow, and I called to him, 'Come on, one last effort.' And it brings the tears to my eyes even now, seeing him straighten up, and come charging back down the pitch, and when the ball comes over for the corner he goes charging out to block the shot, and he blocks it, and it hits him where it hurts most. 'Yes!' I'm thinking, 'cos Moose hacks it away, but the whistle's gone.

What for?

Their ref, he's pointing to the penalty spot.

All hell breaks loose. Giffy and Johnny G, they're rushing up to the ref and screaming at him, it's no penalty, it never touched his hand, it hit him in the knackers. Andy P's still down. He's curled up in a ball, nursing himself. Rolls over on to his knees.

'I'll take the kick,' he says.

'You can't,' I shouted back, 'it's a penalty to them.'

That stung him.

He forgets he's hurt. He scampers up to his feet and goes charging after their ref. He doesn't argue the toss, he just bawls at him, 'I tell you what you are, sir, you're a cheat.'

And the ref tries to send him off, but by now Stockwell's on and he's red in the face, too, with his moustache bristling, and he's having a go at their ref.

And the crowd, they're jeering and booing.

One of them says in a loud voice, 'What a disgrace they are.'

I think he meant us.

The only person not involved, is Mitch. He's standing quietly by the goalpost, pulling his gloves on tighter. He's got a very serious look on his face.

Shaun comes up, places the ball.

As he walked past me, I said, 'How many penalties do you need before you score one?'

But I knew he was going to score. It was a horrible down feeling.

I noticed the suit bloke with the trophy. He's on his mobile. Looks agitated. One of the Northolt dads' with him. The dad bawls out, 'Ashley are 3–0 up!'

Mitch is standing in the middle of the goal, staring straight into Shaun's eyes.

Shaun steps back, trots up.

Hammers it.

Mitch doesn't move.

The ball smacks straight into his chest, and he catches it.

The groan that went up from the Northolt crowd. It was like one voice. It was beautiful.

Yes! I was on fire.

Stockwell's got his arms in the air, pointing at his wrist.

'That's got to be time,' he's shouting.

But their ref, he takes no notice. He looks at his watch with a frown, ever so careful.

At that moment, I hated that ref more than anyone I've ever hated in my life, and I wanted to show him, I wanted to show him what happens to people who try and cheat.

Mitch boots it up field.

I went racing after that ball. No one was going to beat me to that ball and no one was going to stop me getting it. Their number 4 did get there first, but he was pussying with it. He could see me coming, and he did a little shimmy and got out the way. I ran, and there was Pete running a bit ahead of me. I'm screaming at him, 'Go, go, go!' And he's running, and their defence is all running along with us, but they're not tackling. One bloke sticks his foot in like he's feeling the water in a cold pool, but I just ran through him.

I got to the edge of the box, and I was finished. I could hardly stand up. I knew I ought to cross it for Pete, but I was stuck there in the mud, and I went for the shot. I hammered it, or tried to, but I miss hit it and it went looping up and across. Way behind Pete. Across the box.

Pete throws his arms up in despair.

The ball goes over their centre back.

Away from the keeper.

And then I saw this beautiful sight.

On his own, blind side of the whole defence, ten metres out, was Danny Barker.

Everyone, but everyone, they'd forgotten about him.

The ball dropped.

Time stood still.

The centre back, the fullback, the keeper, are all scrambling back.

'Stick it in!' I bawled.

Danny shut his eyes, and hurled himself.

I don't know which bit of him got there first. But the ball hit him on the very top of the head.

At that moment the centre back, the fullback and the keeper arrived. Danny went down, with defenders all over him.

But the ball.

The ball!

That beautiful ball, it popped up off the top of Danny's head, up in the air, high in the air in a gentle arc, up and over the other fullback, looping towards the goal. Number 4, he's scrambling back, looking back over his shoulder. Shaun's coming the other way.

'Darren's ball!' shouts the number 4.

Shaun pulls up.

The ball's dropping.

Number 4 turns. He's got it covered. He goes to head it. His feet get tangled. He stretches, he slips. His feet are coming this way, his head's going that way, he's down flat on his bum, and that ball.

That beautiful ball dropped just under the bar, and rattled against the back of the net, and bounced down, and nestled in the corner, like a fish in a keep net.

I went mad. I was screaming. I don't know what I was screaming. I was bouncing up and down. I had my fists in the air.

The bloke in the suit, he's got the trophy under his arm, ready to put it back in the car.

On the sideline, there's Miss Gilbey and Stockwell hugging each other, and Julie and Heather and Bobby and Moxy and Kenny all in a knot hugging and jumping and shouting.

I went tearing up to Danny, who's on all fours, in a heap of defenders. Danny's staring with wide open eyes at the ball lying in the net.

I grabbed Danny's big head, and I kissed him square on the fat mouth.

Someone was shouting, 'Chris!'

I looked up.

One of their blokes is running away with the ball at his feet. I stopped hugging.

Bobby's screaming from the sideline, 'Get back!'

The ref had disallowed the goal. I still don't know what for.

There wasn't time to complain.

I ran back.

I'm not that fast a runner, and I was knackered, but this time, I ran. I put my head down and sprinted.

Everyone thought we'd scored, so we'd started hugging and jumping and falling on each other. We were all over the place.

Stockwell's chasing back too, down the touchline. He's urging me on. He's got this mad smile on his face, and he's shouting, 'Time!' and pointing at the ref, and then at his wrist. The ref's chasing the play too, running with these high dainty steps, with his motorcycle boots on, and he pretends he hasn't seen Stockwell, but all the time he's running, he's gazing at his watch, squinting, like he's got this game timed down to the last second.

They went through us like a knife through butter.

They were 5 on 3.

Giffy held them up on the edge of the area, tackling one, but the ball ran loose to one of the runners, and Jim fouled him, but the ref didn't blow, 'cos the ball ran loose on the edge of the area and this guy slid it through, and guess who's unmarked on the edge of the area?

Shaun.

Mitch is stumbling back across the goal 'cos he was committed to the first guy. Shaun is so cool. He draws his foot back for the side foot into the empty net.

I took him out.

From behind, I took him out: leg, ball, the lot.

I had my studs up, and I caught him.

The whistle goes, a real loud one.

Shaun twists out from under me. He's got hold of my shirt by the neck.

'You dirty b***. You could have broken my leg.'

I wriggled my arms clear, pushed him off, scrambled up to my feet.

My head was on fire, my heart was pounding. It was like a big hot rock bursting up in my throat.

The ref was trotting over, reaching for his pocket.

I didn't hang around.

I ran straight past the ref, going the other way.

'*That* was a penalty,' I said.

'Hey, young man!'

I didn't stop. I didn't even turn to look. I knew what Angel Mouth was doing. Another yellow card, then a red.

'Number 10, you're off – disgraceful tackle!' he shouted.

I got to the sideline.

Stockwell was almost bursting with rage.

He couldn't speak.

He had to look away.

I couldn't bear it.

The injustice of it, the cheating unfairness of their ref disallowing Danny's goal and then them coming straight back up the pitch. It's like a big burning thing inside you. You want to set the record straight. You know you've all worked so hard and you can still be cheated out of it.

My leg was on fire. I looked down. Where I'd fouled Shaun, I'd got a graze all the way from my shin to my knee. There were little spots of blood pushing up from the raw skin, in among the mud and grass bits.

'Come on, Mitch,' I called.

He doesn't reply. Doesn't look over. He's focusing on the ball, which is on the penalty spot.

Shaun again.

'Miss it,' I whispered.

Shaun trots up and welts it. High and fast and right. Mitch throws himself – high and fast and right. He twists in mid-air and reaches out with his wrong hand, his left hand, and he gets his fingers to it, and the ball flips off his hand and on to the bar – *slap* – comes out, looping. Pete's there, he jumps – go on! – but it drops about a centimetre over his head.

Shaun's waiting there on the penalty spot. It seems like for ever it takes for that ball to arrive, and when it does arrive back to him, he gets his head on it full flush, one of those clumping headers with all the power of his braced neck. It's like our defence is all rooted to the spot.

The ball flies like a shell, *whack*, into the back of the net.

A split second of silence, then they start. Their whole team running and dancing and jumping and shouting and zooming like aeroplanes. And us, we're like corpses.

It's agony.

I sink to my knees. The mud feels warm.

Moose has got his head in his hands.

Andy P is flat on his back, chest heaving.

Mitch sits on his bum, propped on his hands behind him, shaking his head.

Giffy grabs the ball out of the net, kicks it high in the air.

The suit bloke has the trophy back out of the car, wiping it with the back of his sleeve.

Stockwell has turned his back on the pitch. He's shaking his head. Miss Gilbey has her hand on his arm, puzzled, asking what it all means.

Stockwell turns round, bellows, waving his fists, 'Come on, there's still time!'

And I was stood there, choked, because I'm off the pitch now. It feels like being paralysed. You just want to get out there and run and die for your team, and you can't. There's nothing at all you can do.

Nothing anyone can do.

As soon as we kicked off, the ref blew for full-time.

And that was the draggiest, downest, bitter-twisted feeling I ever felt.

We should have won. We could have won.

And we'd been robbed.

Andy P picked the ball up, and goes tearing after their ref, and holds the ball out to him.

'Here,' he goes. 'I think this is yours.'

The ref looks surprised, says, 'I think it's your home game, so it's your ball, isn't it?'

'No, sir, it's yours. 'Cos you were the man of the match.'

And Andy P tossed him the ball.

The ref had to catch it. So he's stood there holding it. He looked white. Drained.

I don't remember much about what happened then. We trooped off. We were gutted. Shaun the Striker shook hands with all of us.

He was so generous.

'Bad luck, lads,' he said. 'You were tough to break down.'

'You still didn't win,' I think I said to him. But he'd run on. To have his photo taken.

They filed up to get the trophy.

The photographer from the local paper took loads of pictures.

No one took any pictures of us.

We went off and got changed.

I didn't have a shower.

I didn't want to be in the changing-rooms when Northolt came back in.

It's a funny feeling, when you're all sweaty and red and hot and muddy, and you put your clothes on over the top. It feels like you're hiding something and it could all rub off all over everywhere. Like you've messed yourself.

Danny was pulling the shirt off.

After he pulled it off, he stared at it, and then sniffed it.

Andy P slapped him on the shoulder.

'You did OK, Dazzer.'

'Yeah,' shouts Mitch from across the hut. 'That was a great goal.'

'Shame about the ref,' said Moose.

'Come on, Danny,' I said, 'let's split.'

We got outside.

Miss Gilbey was there with the girls.

She ran over to Danny and hugged him.

'You were wonderful,' she said. 'And you, Chrissy. I've always hated football, but that was fantastic. You all played so well, and tried so hard.'

That was like twisting the knife.

I tried a smile.

It came out like a snarl.

Stockwell was standing with his back to us, about ten metres away, scuffing his feet, head down.

I couldn't say anything. I said to Danny, 'Come on, Danny, your mum'll be wondering where you are.'

We trudged off.

'Chrissy! Hang on.'

It was Stockwell, puffing over.

He had the ball. He said, 'Did you put your shirt in the bag?'

I nodded.

He said to Danny, 'Well done, lad. You did very well.'

Stockwell wanted to say something else, but he couldn't.

I said, 'Sorry, sir. We nearly did it.'

'Nearly?' he crowed. He was almost shouting. His eyes were wild. 'Nearly? You did do it. That pathetic excuse for a ref played twelve minutes' injury time! Twelve minutes! He would have played till Christmas, until they scored.'

And then he had to turn away. He was nearly
choking with rage and disappointment.

Extra time: a proper goal

As soon as we got out of the school, Danny stopped trudging. He started humming to himself and trotting along and kicking at stones and nodding imaginary headers.

'Why are you so happy?' I said.

He slowed down, dragged his feet.

'It was a good game,' he said.

'No it wasn't,' I snapped back. 'We didn't win.'

Danny thought for a minute. He was counting on his fingers.

'Yes we did. And I scored, didn't I?'

It was on the tip of my tongue to say, 'No, you didn't score. That cheating ref disallowed it.'

But, I didn't say that.

I bit it back. I made myself smile.

I slapped him on the back.

'Yes,' I said. 'You scored a great goal –'

'A proper goal,' he said.

'That's right. That was a proper goal all right.'

Danny walked on. He was bouncing on his feet.

'You know what?' he said.

'Surprise me.'

'The goal nets have got orange string to hold them up.'

'That's right!' I said. 'They have. Come on. Chris to Danny.'

And I ran, and he chased me, and I pretend-crossed the ball, and he pretend-nodded the pretend ball into a pretend goal, and we both shouted:

'Goal!'

We ran like that all the way home.

Egghead
Steve May

'And then it starts going through your mind again, all the things Egghead could do, and wondering where he is, 'cos he can't be nowhere, he's somewhere out there, and he's not finished yet. He's not going to stop now. He's going to do something else. He's going to do something worse.'

Billy wants to be 'in' with the gang. It's his idea to drop the egg on the man on the beach. He doesn't think the man will strike back. But now, Egghead is after him. Which way will Billy turn? To Kevin, the gang leader, the devil in his life, or Pip, the beautiful angel, ready to save him?

A brilliant, dark psychological thriller.

15, Going on 20

Steve May

Sixteen year old Laura is on holiday with her mother in Greece where she befriends the Skytours rep, twenty-two year old Audrey. Impressed by Audrey's vivacity and experience, Laura joins her on her escapades, lying about her age and recreating her past.

When Audrey's best friend arrives and they drop Laura, she decides to sample the exciting adult lifestyle of bars and discos on her own. Without Audrey's protection and made even more vulnerable by her own lies, Laura finds herself in some tricky situations . . .